TABLE OF CONTENTS

*Too my wonderful editor, Mel.
With out u, my commas wood all be in the wrong
spots. I think this buk is rite now, thanks!*

ACKNOWLEDGMENTS

Thank you to all the fans of the Kisses Series. It is because of you all that I am able to tell these stories. I have the best job ever and it is all thanks to you!

CHAPTER ONE

I looked up from my book and took in a big breath of fresh sea air. This was what a vacation was supposed to look like. White sand turned into pale blue water that slowly darkened as it stretched out toward the horizon. A tiny sailboat floated across the view, its yellow sails bright and cheerful against the sky. Behind me, green palms fluttered in the warm breeze.

I took a sip of the latest concoction from the bar and then set it down in the sand beside me. It was sweet with some sort of fruit juice and had a giant paper umbrella sticking out of the top. I closed my eyes, letting the warm sun shine down on me for a moment before starting the next chapter. This was so much better than my normal Novembers in Chicago. A girl could get used to tropical vacations like this.

I heard the soft sound of feet on sand and I turned

to see two of my favorite people walking toward me. I grinned and sat up on the edge of my lounge chair and waved to my best friend and her son. Maddy walked slowly, trying, and from the irritated look on her face, failing to keep sand out of the walking boot wrapped around her foot. Tyler, her eleven-year-old son, grinned and hurried over, leaving his mother behind.

"Hi, Aunt Olivia," he greeted me enthusiastically as he stopped next to my chair. I couldn't help but smile back at him. It was the first time in weeks that I had seen him legitimately happy. He was having a rough time making friends in a new school and transitioning to a single-parent household. I had hoped bringing him on vacation would help raise his spirits, and judging by the grin on his face, it was working.

"Hey, Tyler," I replied. I loved that he called me Aunt even though we weren't really related. His mother and I worked closely together, and he had decided I deserved the aunt moniker the first day we met. I didn't have any siblings, so the possibility of me being a real aunt anytime soon was zilch. I loved Tyler like he was my own. "You having fun?"

"This resort is amazing. Did you know there's a free bowling alley? And pizza is served all day?" Tyler ran a clumsy hand through his disheveled brown hair and grinned. His arms were too long for his body since he was in the middle of yet another growth spurt. "We're still on for jet-skis in an hour, right?"

"Of course! I promised, didn't I?" I responded, scooting over on my lounge chair to make space for

Maddy. She sat down gratefully, stretching the awkward black cast out in front of her.

"I really appreciate you taking him, Liv," Maddy said once Tyler finished making an overzealous gesture of excitement. "I feel awful that I can't do it. Stupid ice."

She glared down at the boot as if the inanimate object could feel shame. She had slipped on some ice outside our office two days before the trip and had broken her foot. The doctor had given her a walking boot, so at least she was slightly more mobile and able to enjoy our trip. She was being a good sport about it, but she was obviously not terribly comfortable.

"Maddy, you know I'm more than happy to do it. I just wish you could come with us!" I put my hand on her shoulder and she shrugged. I winked at Tyler and told his mother, "I promise to do as many dangerous things as possible. I'm expecting broken bones, but we'll have a great time."

Maddy shot me a dirty look and Tyler laughed.

"I know where you sleep," she threatened. "And I know all the things that scare you."

I laughed. Maddy was only joking. Well, mostly joking. She was very protective of her son, especially since the divorce. I had no doubt that if I brought him back injured, I would have matching injuries within the hour.

"Can we go over to the jet-skis now?" Tyler asked, his eyes dancing with excitement. "I already have my swimsuit on and I'm ready."

"I have to go check my email first. And change." I answered. Tyler frowned and I held up my hands to block his accusing look. "Hey, someone has to work to get us these lavish vacations."

"Fine." Tyler crossed his arms and tried to pout, but he was still too eager about the upcoming jet-ski adventure to make it convincing.

"That reminds me, I have the waivers for you in our room. I'll go get them," Maddy said as I rose to collect my things. I eyed her cast and raised my eyebrows at her. The doctor had said to try and stay off her foot as much as possible.

"Can Tyler get them?" I asked her.

Maddy gave a soft sigh of frustration. She'd had the cast for three days and was already tired of being babied because of her foot. "Not if you want them signed."

"Can I wait for Aunt Liv by the dock, then?" Tyler asked, bouncing on his toes and looking past us down the beach. I could just make out the dock where we were supposed to get our jet-skis with a small storage shed next to it. Eagerness and excitement radiated off of Tyler as though he were a small sun of anticipation. His mom looked at him for a moment, considering the idea, and then nodded. The resort was small with good security. He would be safe waiting for me there.

"All right, but you stay out of the water until Olivia gets there." She paused with a stern face until Tyler enthusiastically agreed. She smiled at his back as he took off down the beach to go look at the jet-skis. "He is so excited about this. Thank you, again. I'll go get the waivers and meet you at your room."

I pointedly looked at her cast. "And then?"

Maddy rolled her eyes. "And then I'll stay off it.

Go get a massage or something."

I held my hand out to help her up. She was only about seven years older than I was, but I still needed to use a fair amount of strength to get her to stand. She looked tired, so I was glad I could get her energetic son out of her hair for a while. Being a single mother, even with a fairly self-sufficient kid, was not an easy thing, especially when trying to keep up with him on a broken foot.

We walked slowly through the elaborate lobby of Island Oasis Resort until we reached the elevator to our rooms. I was on the third floor while she was on the second. There were only thirty rooms in the entire resort, making it small and cozy. The goal of the resort was to not only be an exclusive luxury destination, but also to be one of the most ecologically friendly hotels in the world. It was the newest line from Diamond Hotels, and Island Oasis Resort was to be their flagship hotel.

Once inside my room, I opened up my laptop and let it power on as I stripped and changed into a full-piece swimsuit and board shorts. I logged in and started going through my daily assault of emails. Despite considering this trip to be a vacation, I was really here on business. This was a working trip.

My room was one of the premier suites, which made sense because the resort was trying to woo me. The resort officially opened in December, but they had invited several travel companies for a free weekend retreat in order to promote it. I had a large bedroom with a massive king-sized bed, as well as a reception area with a large desk where I could work.

They had even provided me with everything I would need to work while on the island. A top-of-the-line printer/fax machine rested on a small, wheeled table with a full collection of office supplies next to the desk.

Island Oasis Resort was courting my travel company, Dream Vacations. My business was arranging personalized vacations and specialty travel. We offered all the convenience and discounts of the big website travel agencies, but with the personal touches only a person could give. In two years of business, I now had six consultants working from home full time, a tech guy, an accountant, two office employees and Maddy. And the best part, the part that I was most proud of, was that my business was rated by Forbes as one of the fastest-growing companies to keep an eye on. My main competition had thought we wouldn't make a dime, so I'd say we weren't doing too badly.

It hadn't been easy. I had gotten off to a very rocky start, no thanks to a certain businessman named Logan Hayes, but once Maddy had joined me, the business took off. It was a dream come true. I had put my heart and soul into the company, and my success reflected my desire to see it succeed.

A knock on the door drew my attention, and I left the last email unopened to go see who was there. I wasn't expecting anyone but Maddy. Waiting politely at the door was a man in the crisp, blue hotel uniform.

"Ms. Olivia Statler?" he asked. I nodded and he handed me a white envelope. I thanked him and he nodded respectfully before turning back down the hallway.

The envelope was made of expensive-looking white paper and felt heavy enough to hold something important. I left the door open a crack so Maddy could walk directly in, and carefully undid the seal of the envelope. My location wasn't a secret, but I certainly wasn't expecting any mail to be delivered here.

Dear Ms. Statler,

While we are not willing to negotiate control of the company, Travel, Inc. is willing to increase our original offer by 10%. Travel, Inc. would, of course, have sole ownership. Acquiring your business is something we are very interested in...

When I scanned quickly to the bottom of the letter to see the signature of Logan Hayes, my blood started to boil.

Logan Hayes.

My hand clenched around the letter, crumpling it into a ball. I hated that man. No, "hate" wasn't a strong enough word. I despised him with every fiber of my being. Not only had he led me on romantically, but he was responsible for almost destroying my company. His company, Travel, Inc., was the biggest online travel company in the world. His father was the CEO, but he and his brother were the guys who really ran it. There had been negotiations to purchase my company when I was first starting out, and Logan had seemed incredibly interested. However, he had quickly shown his true colors. Logan Hayes was the scum of the earth.

The letter was just the latest in a series of offers to acquire Dream Vacations. Now that my business was actually successful, they wanted it. Travel, Inc.'s initial rejection had nearly destroyed me when I was low on start-up capital. They had left me to dangle and struggle while making it impossible for me to find other investors. But I had survived, and now that Dream Vacations was successful, Travel, Inc. wanted it again. This latest offer was tempting, but there was no way I would ever let Logan Hayes or his family anywhere near my business.

I would rather let it burn in a fiery blaze than sell it to him.

Not that it was going to. Dream Vacations was doing better than I could have imagined. We were turning profits that made my previous salaries look like play money. Plus, I loved having the freedom of running my own company. The decisions were all mine to make. I didn't have to answer to anyone, except occasionally Maddy. If I didn't like the way things were being done, I had the power to change them. Taking the offer from Travel, Inc. would make me very, very wealthy, but I would lose the freedom that I loved. This company was my life. It wouldn't go up for sale no matter how much they promised.

I was about to throw the crumpled offer into the trash when I decided that simply tossing it wasn't enough. I sat down at the desk and began ripping it into tiny pieces and putting them in a return envelope. I didn't stop when Maddy knocked and then let herself in.

"What's that?" she asked, coming over to the desk.

"Another offer from Travel, Inc.," I answered and put the last piece of the offer in the envelope.

"Are you accepting it?" She sounded shocked. She had been there for the aftermath of my association with Logan Hayes and Travel, Inc. Besides that, she technically owned part of the company and would have to agree to it as well.

I blew my nose and then stuffed the used tissue in the envelope before sealing it. I held it up to hand it off to Maddy.

"You know I'm not mailing that, right? That's gross." Maddy gave me one of those disgusted, disapproving looks that only a mother can give. She did not take the envelope.

"You're right. It's terribly unprofessional," I conceded with a sigh, setting the letter on the desk. "And besides, it just isn't enough to convey just how certainly he is not getting my company."

After what he had done to my company two years ago, a snot-filled envelope was more than he deserved.

ॐ❦ ❦ॐ

CHAPTER TWO

Two Years Earlier...

I took a deep breath, smoothed the front of my skirt, and stepped into the office of Travel, Inc.'s Chief Operation Officer. If this worked, I would have the funding and connections to make my dreams a reality. I was going to do the job I wanted, instead of the job I hated. If this meeting went well, Travel, Inc. would add Dream Vacations' services to their already massive empire. I would have all the resources of the biggest travel website to make my concierge travel planning the best it could possibly be.

The last two months of my life I had dedicated to getting my business up and running. The computer program that was the heart of Dream Vacations had been a pet project of mine over the past year and a half, and now I was finally ready to use it. I had waltzed out of my terrible computer programming job the minute I had finished it with a smile on my face.

I now had the website, the business plan, and the connections, but I needed more funding. Advertisements were expensive, and concierge travel planning wasn't something that the average person considered within their budget. I wanted to change that mindset, but I needed advertisements to do so. Word of mouth was helping, but I needed access to a bigger market. I had used up all my savings and was in limbo for a business loan. With their resources, Travel, Inc. could change everything. If they decided to purchase either my program or my entire business, I would be a winner.

The corner office was large and ornate. It was bigger and nicer than my apartment. Floor-to-ceiling windows overlooked the city with a large desk in the center that probably cost more than my car. A handsome man reclined in the plush leather chair behind the shiny desk. I did a double take as I came in. I had seen Logan Hayes in pictures, but he was even cuter in person. He ran a hand through his messy, honey-colored hair and smiled. I had the sudden wish to tangle my fingers in those short, loose curls.

"It's a pleasure to meet you, Olivia," he greeted me, rising to shake my hand. A tingle went up my arm as his hand squeezed mine. He gestured to one of the two chairs opposite his desk. "Please, have a seat."

"It's very nice to meet you as well, Mr. Hayes," I replied. My voice only shook at the first word, but I hoped he hadn't noticed. I sat nervously, smoothing my non-wrinkled skirt again before setting a copy of my proposal on the desk. Despite my best intentions, I had already crinkled the edges with my nervous grip.

"Call me Logan, please. I've been over your proposal, and I love the concept. There's a couple of things that would need to be changed, but overall, I really think the concept is amazing." He leaned back in his chair and watched my reaction. His eyes were warm, chocolate-caramel pools that seemed to absorb me. Being the sole object of his attention was distracting enough to make me forget how to breathe. I wondered if all his clients felt this way in his presence.

"Thank you, sir," I finally sputtered. "I've worked really hard on it. Having the resources of Travel, Inc. would make it exponentially easier, and far more viable."

His lips perked up in a small smile at my nervousness. I hoped he found it endearing, because I was having a hard time concentrating with his eyes on me. It didn't help that he was exactly my type.

"I agree," he said, leaning forward and putting his elbows on the desk. "What are you hoping to get out of this meeting?"

My lips suddenly felt very dry and I had to fight the urge to lick them. "Honestly? I would love it if you decided to purchase my company and let me run it under Travel, Inc.'s banner. A big sticking point for me here is that I get to continue to work with this. I have put my heart and soul into this program and the business. I won't sell it just to walk away."

"It's your baby. I can understand that," he said, sitting back in his chair again. He looked thoughtful for a moment as a small smile crept onto his face. He was wearing an unbuttoned, light gray suit jacket. It accented the width of his shoulders and the lean build of muscle underneath the fabric. He belonged in a magazine. "I have a couple of questions about your business before I bring the proposal to my father," he said, never taking those delicious brown eyes off me.

"Your father?" I frowned slightly. I was under the impression he was in charge.

He pointed to the name plate on the edge of his desk. Logan Hayes, Senior COO.

"I'm just the COO. My father is the official CEO of the company. A transaction like this will require his approval, so I want to make sure I present it accurately," he explained. "I really think that your company will be a major asset, and I want to present it as such."

I nodded, wiping my sweaty hands on my skirt. "Okay. Do you think he'll like it?"

Logan grinned. "I wouldn't bring it to him if I didn't."

His smile made my insides heat. He had to be the company's secret weapon for negotiations. When he looked at me, I felt like I was the center of his world. I was the only thing that mattered with those dark brown eyes absorbing me. I could stay in those eyes forever, basking in his attention.

I could already feel myself falling head-over-heels for him, which was ridiculous. He wouldn't be interested in me. This was a business tactic to warm me up to his negotiations. I merely represented a small company asking to become part of Travel, Inc.'s empire. I could only imagine the level of charm he probably bestowed upon bigger-name clients.

"I do have to ask something, though," he said. "Do you have any other investors who will complicate a transition to Travel, Inc.?"

I shook my head. "Not currently. There are a couple of other companies that I have met with, much like this one, but no forms have been signed yet." I didn't tell him just how interested a couple of them really had been. I had two other companies completely ready to combine my business with theirs, but Travel, Inc.'s budget blew all of them out of the water. The business prospects of joining with the biggest travel company in the world were the best I could hope for at this point. Logan and Travel, Inc. were the ones I wanted.

"That's good to hear." His smiled widened, and my heartbeat sped up. I couldn't imagine a sexier smile than the one lighting up his face. He played with a pen on his desk, his eyes never leaving mine. "If you want to continue to be a part of this project, I have some ideas for improvement, if you have the time."

"That would be wonderful," I gushed. "I'd love to hear your thoughts, and I have some plans that I think Travel, Inc. would really benefit from." I'd have rescheduled a date with Brad Pitt for this opportunity. One of the most successful men in business, specifically my field, was offering to go over ideas for improvement. Not to mention the effect he was having on my pulse. I wouldn't have missed this for the world.

He chuckled softly and pressed a key on the phone resting on his desk. "Virginia, hold my calls."

"Yes, sir," a voice replied through the intercom.

Logan stood and straightened his jacket as he came

around the desk. He sat in the chair next to me, and my heart rate shot up again. By the end of this meeting, I would have had my cardio for the day

"It's easier to talk to you over here. The desk just gets in the way," he explained nonchalantly. I nodded nervously. Our knees were almost touching here. My mind was imagining all the wonderful things I wanted to do with him. Tangling my fingers in those honey curls. The way those broad shoulders would look without clothes on. The touch of his skin against mine.

"Right," I stuttered.

Focus, I told myself. *He's a billionaire. He could have anyone. He's had supermodels. He's not interested in you. This is just a business tactic.*

Flirting and charm were as deadly of weapons in the business world as swords and arrows.

He smiled again, and those brown eyes threatened to swallow me whole. "So, how do you plan on keeping work hours down? Personalizing someone's travel is difficult and time-consuming."

"I have a form for prospective clients to fill out. I then run it through a computer program that I created specifically with travel customization in mind. The program is actually the basis for my company. Using the customer entries, user ratings, pricing, and some other variables, I created the program to come up with a number of basic vacation plans," I explained. I tried not to blush when he nodded encouragingly. "Then, with that base, it's easy to customize the trip as needed. Most people actually want very similar vacations, so it's not as much of a

time sink as you might think."

"I see," he said, nodding once more. A curl fell across his forehead. "Is the program's vacation planning offered for free initially? Or is there a cost involved?"

"Right now, I'm offering it for free just to gain word of mouth. I'm working on a modified version that will allow very basic trip-planning services for free, with the option of upgrading to the better packages," I told him. I loved talking about my company. I'd taken such a leap of faith to quit my day job and take this risk, but I was happier than I had been in months. I knew success was within my grasp.

"Interesting," he said. His knee bumped mine, and I felt an electric rush into my lower belly. I wanted to brush that curl off his forehead so badly my fingers ached. "What else do you have in the works?"

I grinned and proceeded to explain my plans for the future. Logan listened attentively and asked questions that made me stop and think. He was incredibly astute, and his business reputation was undeniably well deserved. In the course of an hour, he had found several small flaws and offered solutions to problems I hadn't foreseen in addition to ones I was struggling with.

"That is the perfect solution," I said for the umpteenth time. He saw the holes in my fledgling business with an eagle eye, pointing them out and helping me think of the solution. I was in awe and completely crushing on him. Not only was he good-looking, smart, and rich--he was sweet too. I never once felt he was picking on me; rather, I felt he was

going out of his way to help me.

The intercom buzzed, diverting his attention away from me. He smiled apologetically and pressed the button.

"I'm very sorry, sir, but Aiden Hayes is here," the woman on the on the other end stated. Logan looked disappointed.

"Of course he is," he replied. He let go of the button and sighed. "Well, Olivia, it was a pleasure meeting with you."

"Likewise," I said, rising from my seat. My legs felt heavy. I wondered just how long we had been sitting there.

The door to his office opened, and a slicker version of Logan walked in. He was just as tall with a similar build, but with a slightly leaner frame. His hair was the same warm honey-gold color, but instead of Logan's wild curls, he had smoothed his back. He looked richer, if that were possible.

"Logan, you missed the meeting," he said, giving me the once-over. I smiled nervously, but his face stayed blank. He turned to Logan and gave him a look that I couldn't read.

"I'm aware." Logan put his hand on my shoulder and walked me to the door of his office. It was a sweet gesture, but his touch made my body sing with want. I was dying for him to touch me all over. He paused with his hand on the door. "Perhaps we can get drinks later? I'd love to continue our discussion."

I grinned, feeling a blush settle in my cheeks. I felt like the captain of the football team had just asked me to homecoming. "That would be great. You have my

number on the proposal."

He beamed, letting go of my shoulder to shake my hand. We both held it a second longer than was necessary. I giggled as I realize neither of us had let go, then ducked out the door before I could embarrass myself further. He couldn't possibly be interested in me. He just liked my business idea and was a natural flirt.

"Drinks, Logan?" I heard his brother through the door. "You never take clients out for drinks."

"Not now, Aiden," came Logan's reply. The secretary guarding his office was giving me the evil eye, so I stepped away from the door before I could hear more. I couldn't stop the grin from spreading across my face as I walked back to the elevator to get to the lobby. I was going to have drinks with Logan Hayes tonight. Things were going better than I could have possibly hoped.

CHAPTER THREE

Present Day

Maddy laughed and scooted the snot-filled envelope off my desk and into a trash can. "You have a pen?" she asked, setting the unsigned waiver on the desk. I fished her one out of a drawer and went to open the last email in my inbox. It was my daily news and I nearly punched my laptop screen because of the headline article.

"What?" Maddy asked as I made an angry growl at the offending article. I turned the screen to face her. Logan Hayes and his brother's smiling faces filled the screen with the headline "Hayes Family Donates Millions to Mayoral Candidate."

"Ah, Logan Hayes again. He is a good-looking man," she said appreciatively, taking in the image. I glared at her and she clarified, "A jerk, but a handsome one."

She was, of course, right. Maddy was always right. Logan Hayes was incredibly good-looking. It was part of

his charm. He was tall with broad shoulders and an easy smile that was made to be photographed. Both he and his brother had short honey-colored curls; Logan's were always messy while Aiden's tended to be slicked back and controlled. They could have been movie stars with their looks.

And acting ability, I thought snidely to myself.

"You aren't helping." I glared at Maddy as she continued to inspect the handsome men. She just laughed and handed me the freshly-signed waiver. The paper crinkled slightly in my hand; seeing his picture was making my vision go red again and I was taking it out on another piece of paper.

"You should get going. Tyler's probably worn a hole down to China with his pacing." She stopped looking at the evil photograph and went to the window, peering out at the ocean view like she might see Tyler out there. "I really, really appreciate you taking him jet-skiing. And for bringing him on this trip. He's been having a rough time, and he still hasn't made any friends-"

"Maddy," I interrupted, standing up and putting a hand on her shoulder, "I know. I'm really glad he could come with us. He's actually smiling and talking today."

"Isn't it great?" she turned, hope in her eyes. The past year had been hard on her and Tyler. Things had gone downhill with her ex-husband, and she and Tyler had been forced to move. Things at Tyler's new school weren't going well. He was a shy, geeky eleven-year-old middle schooler in a new school system. I hadn't seen him smile like this in months.

"We're going to have a blast," I told Maddy. "This whole week, we're going to have a good time. Maybe with a little bit of sun and fun, he'll go back happier and be able to make some friends."

"I hope so. He's just lost all his confidence, you

know?" Maddy peered out the window again, eyes going past the ocean and back to her problems at home. "I just worry about him. I can't believe his father did this to us. To him."

"It's not your fault, and Tyler knows that." I turned her to face me, giving her a version of the speech I gave her at home whenever she felt guilty about the divorce and her son. "Tyler's whole world just crumbled around him. With his dad running off, the divorce, moving, and then just the fact that he's eleven and in a new school, life is going to be rough. But he's going to be okay. This trip-and getting to hang out with people who love him even when his voice cracks-is going to be good for him."

"I just feel like a bad mom," Maddy said quietly, not meeting my gaze. My heart squeezed in my chest for my best friend.

"You are anything but a bad mom, Maddy." I hugged her close. "You love your son. You are doing everything you can to help him with this. He's a good kid. He'll make it through. Middle school is rough for just about everybody."

Maddy hugged me back. I could feel her pulling strength into herself again. She never let Tyler see this side of her. Only me. She wanted to be strong for Tyler, and I, in turn, was strong for her. She let me go and made sure I had the waiver in my hand. "I feel better. Do you?"

"Yes. And now that you've managed to effectively distract me from my rage toward Logan Hayes, I'm going to go meet your son," I said as she gave me a cheesy grin. She had known I would comfort her and forget my anger. She was such a mom. I shook my head at her and smiled. "Go get that massage. My treat."

"Thanks, boss. You two have fun. And don't let him show off too much," she warned, walking me to the door.

"He's a junior high school boy. I don't think that's

going to be possible," I responded, trying to keep a straight face as we stepped out into the hallway. "If there's a cute girl on the beach, I'm completely doomed." Maddy's laugh echoed down the hall as I headed off toward the dock to meet Tyler.

∞∞ ∞∞

CHAPTER FOUR

I walked quickly up the path to the dock where Tyler was supposed to meet me. He was standing patiently next to the storage shed, petting a dog and talking to a man whose back was to me. I admired the back of the attractive male form for a moment, taking in the broad shoulders and muscled frame under a skintight rash guard shirt. His board shorts were low slung and accentuated a perfect ass. I hoped that this delightful male specimen would be joining us and that his front was as attractive as his back. I could use a little vacation romance.

"Hey, Tyler," I called out as I approached. "You ready?"

Tyler raised his hand and grinned at me. The man he was talking to turned around and I nearly ate asphalt as I momentarily forgot how to walk. His

23

front was as handsome as his back, all right. But that was because he was also Logan Hayes.

"Olivia Statler," he greeted me with a smile. "It's a pleasure to see you again."

"What the hell are you doing here?" I sputtered, trying to keep my temper in check and mostly failing as I pretended I hadn't just tripped. I hoped neither of them noticed the bright red blush I could feel spreading across my cheeks. I smiled and smoothly joined the two of them next to the shed. Despite my dislike and history with Logan, I could be somewhat diplomatic. Hopefully.

"Aunt Liv, Logan is going jet-skiing too," Tyler informed me. He had apparently missed the venom in my voice toward Logan, and was now smiling happily at the dog in front of him.

"You are, are you?" I asked, forcing my face into something I hoped passed for pleasant instead of angry. "Awesome."

Logan flashed me an easy smile. It was a smile that was made to make women's insides flutter, but for me, it just made my temper flare. This man had nearly ruined me. He nearly destroyed my future with that charming smile and hadn't even bothered to call. I wondered just how many other unsuspecting women he had charmed into failure with that grin.

"Plus, we found this dog here. Isn't he awesome?" Tyler looked up at me, his hand still on the dog's head. It was a brown mutt with white paws and a white splotch on his chest. He wasn't an ugly dog, but he certainly wasn't going to win any dog shows. Judging by the thinness in the dog's ribs and the state of his fur, he was one of the local strays. I had heard they liked to hang out near the tourist areas of the island because they usually could find food.

"Yeah, he looks like a good dog, Tyler. I'm going to go get us some life jackets and turn in your waiver." I let the fake smile drop as soon as I was behind Tyler. Of all people on all the possible islands, Logan Hayes had to be on my vacation island. And if he was jet-skiing here, then he was staying at this resort. Not just visiting from one of his various mansions. No, he was probably with one of the travel agencies touring the resort. That would just be my luck. I would have to see him the entire week.

I handed the waiver to a hotel employee sitting at a desk by the dock. He went into the storage shed and pulled out two life jackets and handed me the key to a jet-ski.

"Do you need any instructions? We offer free beginner lessons," he asked in a thick accent as I shrugged into my life jacket.

"We're good, actually. I've done this since I was a kid and I was here yesterday to practice," I told him. He checked a list and smiled. I had actually stopped by the day before to find out how a jet-ski could be environmentally friendly. The ones at the resort were a brand new type of watercraft that used an electric engine. They looked a little different and so I had to try it out. The smooth ride and quiet of the engine had been fantastic and a big part of how I had been able to convince over-protective Maddy to let me take Tyler.

"Of course, ma'am. Be careful out there today.

The wind is picking up and making waves. If it continues, we'll send a signal out to come back in. Safety is very important here." The man smiled again and nodded to the waiting jet-skis. "Yours is number four."

I nodded and thanked him before going back to Tyler. Logan was on his knees rubbing the tummy of the very happy dog. Tyler was giggling as the dog wiggled and made happy dog noises.

"Let's get your jacket on and get going, Tyler," I said, trying my best to ignore Logan. I had managed to mostly avoid Logan Hayes for almost two years despite working in the same city. I could do it on an island. Tyler stood up quickly and took the life jacket from my hands. I helped him tighten the straps and situate it properly across his bony shoulders.

"So, are you riding with Olivia or driving yourself, Tyler?" Logan asked, apparently not done with talking to Tyler. The dog had rolled back onto its stomach and Logan was scratching his ears.

"I'm not old enough to drive myself yet," Tyler answered with a shrug. I tightened down another strap.

"You'll have fun with her driving, though," Logan mused, his eyes on the dog. "Where are you two headed?"

"None of your business," I said quietly. I hated the way my body was warming at the sight of his muscled arms. Apparently, my body hadn't gotten the memo that we wanted nothing to do with him, because my insides were wanting the something he had given me before.

"The reef over there," Tyler answered at the same time, pointing to a spot a little ways out.

"I've heard there's some good snorkeling there," Logan responded, pretending to not hear my comment. "You have your gear, right?"

"Yup. Aunt Liv even got me better goggles, just for this trip." Tyler pointed to a mesh bag at his feet with his snorkel gear in it. I put my hands on his shoulders and pushed him gently toward the dock.

"Time for us to get going," I told him.

"See you later, Logan!" Tyler waved to the taller man. "Bye, Dog. I'll see you when I get back."

He scratched the ears of the mongrel dog one last time before grabbing his bag and bounding down the dock to our waiting jet-ski

"Have fun," Logan told me, rising gracefully to his feet. Sand stuck to his knees and the hem of his board shorts. It wasn't fair how good those shorts made him look. Why did the man have to be such an ass? I ignored him and hurried after Tyler. I was not going to let the presence of Logan Hayes ruin my vacation. If I just pretended he wasn't there, perhaps he would leave and make it a reality.

Tyler was already on the jet-ski with a grin that threatened to split his face in half. He had been looking forward to going out on the ocean on one of these new jet-skis since he had seen them in the brochure. I stepped off the dock and onto the jet-ski in front of him. Tyler wrapped his skinny arms around my waist and squeezed. I looked back, surprised at the hug.

"You ready?" I asked. He nodded, relaxing his grip

slightly and grinning with excitement.

I revved the engine and took off. He shrieked with delight from behind me as I moved us out into the open water. He whooped as I sped up and bounced us between the waves. I spun us in circles and pushed the jet-ski through its paces. I had spent most of my summers growing up on jet-skis, so I was comfortable even with the new engine.

"Go faster!" Tyler cried out as we bounced over a wave. The wind was making the waves slightly rough, but it wasn't anything I couldn't handle. I hit the gas and sent us hurtling forward. Tyler gripped me tighter and I could feel his laughter rather than hear it.

When Tyler's shrieks of delight started slowing down in frequency, I brought the jet-ski to the edge of the reef. We had been instructed on how to enjoy the reef and still preserve it upon arrival to the resort, so I made sure to keep the jet-ski clear of the delicate coral.

"You ready to snorkel?" I asked, turning off the engine. "There's some cool-looking fish down there."

I pointed down into the clear blue water. A long, thin fish flitted under us and into the safety of the reef.

"Yup," Tyler said, putting his mask over his head. He looked even goofier as the back strap ruffled up his light brown hair like an exotic bird crest. "Are you coming in?"

I shook my head. "Nah, I think I'm going to stay up here and enjoy the sun a little more. If you see a really interesting fish, though, I'll come look."

"Okay." He grinned and jumped into the water.

His orange life jacket bobbed in the waves as it kept him afloat in the clear, blue water.

I took off my own life jacket and hung it from one of the handlebars on the jet-ski. The sun felt so good on my skin. I hated winters in Chicago, and while November didn't technically qualify as winter, it was still too cold and dreary for my taste. Sunshine was so much better.

I leaned back, basking in the rays and listening to the waves. They gently bounced the jet-ski up and down. I could see clouds forming on the horizon. In the distance, there were large whitecaps, but right next to the reef it was relatively quiet. I could hear the soft splashes emitted by Tyler as he swum around looking at fish and the hum of another electric jet-ski. Logan wasn't far from us, bouncing off the water and doing tricks on his own jet-ski. He hit a wave and shot up into the air, the jet-ski rolling in a controlled spin before hitting the water with an easy splash. *Showoff,* I thought, adjusting my sunglasses. I pointedly turned and looked back at Tyler. I did not need to give Logan Hayes an audience.

"Aunt Liv!" Tyler called out, his head popping up from the water. He was on the far side of the small reef. "There's a moray eel over here! You have to come see it!"

"On my way!" I shouted back, starting the engine. I would have to circle around the edge of the reef to get to him since I didn't want to go over it and risk damaging the delicate ecosystem. The jet-ski purred to life and I started the quick jaunt into deeper waters to reach him.

The waves were rougher outside the calm of the reef, but I had been on a jet-ski enough times to know how to ride it. I was almost to Tyler when a rogue wave came out of nowhere and slammed into the jet-ski.

I wasn't ready for it. I felt my body lift from the seat, and suddenly become alarmingly weightless. The last thought through my head before I hit the water was that I had forgotten to put my life jacket back on. Maddy was going to kill me.

CHAPTER FIVE

The world was a beautiful shade of blue, like a robin's egg, but with swirls of white that made me think of cotton candy. I heard Tyler's voice, full of panic and fear, but it was very far away. Pain rushed through me, but it was as if I had never experienced it before and wasn't sure what pain was. My thoughts were dull and foreign as I slowly came back to myself.

"Olivia, can you hear me?" A deep, masculine voice asked. I knew that voice. I loved that voice. No, I hated that voice. That voice belonged to Logan Hayes.

I quickly righted myself so I was no longer looking up at the sky to find myself bobbing in the ocean. Logan had been holding my shoulders to keep me floating above the waves since I didn't have my life jacket on and had been out cold. As I sat up, he released me and I had to remember to tread water to keep my head from going under again. There was a splash as Tyler tossed me my life jacket and I clung to it so I wouldn't have to swim. My head was pounding.

"Of course I can hear you," I answered. I meant to sound cross, but my tongue was sluggish so I just sounded sleepy. "What happened?"

"You hit a wave and flipped," Tyler answered. He was sitting up on our jet-ski, his freckles dark against pale skin. He looked like he might be sick. "It knocked you out."

That would definitely explain the headache. Tyler shifted in his seat, eyes as big as saucers. Maddy would never forgive me when she found out about this. "Are you okay, Tyler?"

"Yeah, I'm fine," he said with a small nod. "Are you okay?"

I did my best to smile up at him, but my whole head was pounding. "I'll be all right. My head just hurts."

"You are pretty damn lucky," Logan admonished. I had almost forgotten that he was there. His jet ski floated peacefully in the water behind him. "Tyler got to you and flipped you onto your back so you wouldn't drown. You're lucky he's a good swimmer and has a good head on his shoulders."

"What are you doing here?" I asked Logan, turning to face him. His blonde curls were plastered to his head from swimming in the water. He looked pissed.

"Tyler was screaming for help. You're lucky to be alive. Why the hell weren't you wearing your life jacket?" Logan glared at me like I had been an idiot. To be fair, I was, but I wasn't about to let him know that I agreed with him.

"I wasn't going that fast. It's not like this was my first time on a jet-ski." I wished I could cross my arms, but that would mean letting go of the life jacket. Logan's frown deepened as his eyes went to my cheek.

Water was dripping from my hair down my face, so I wiped my hand across my cheek to stop the tickling sensation...only it wasn't water. Blood was trickling down my cheek from a cut in my scalp. It wasn't much, but I suddenly had a very strong desire to get out of the water.

"We need to get you back to shore," Logan said with an air of authority. I hated that I immediately wanted to do what he said. "You need to have someone look at your head. You probably have a concussion."

"Thank you, Dr. Hayes," I said as sarcastically as possible. Logan didn't even bat an eyelash. I kicked my feet, propelling myself toward Tyler and the jet-ski.

"Where do you think you're going?" Logan asked, grabbing the life jacket and halting me easily in place.

"To get on my jet-ski and go get my head looked at," I said as calmly as possible. "Are you sure that you're not the one with a head injury?"

"You are not driving. Tyler will take that jet-ski back by himself. You are riding with me."

"Like hell I am!" I pulled at the life jacket to free it from his hands, but his grasp didn't budge an inch. He didn't even sway in the water.

Logan looked at me as though I might be clinically

insane. "You're head is bleeding and you were out for a good couple of minutes. You need someone else to drive."

"I'll ride with Tyler. He can do it," I said stubbornly. The last thing I wanted was to be so close to Logan.

"No," Logan explained patiently, still holding onto my life jacket. "Tyler will be able to handle the jet-ski on his own, but you won't be doing him any favors being off balance. You're riding with me."

"It'll be okay, Aunt Liv. I'll be right behind you. Logan's good on a jet-ski. I saw him. You'll be fine." I looked up at Tyler. He was so pale against the orange of his life jacket that I thought he might pass out at any moment, but he stayed sitting and did his best to smile encouragingly at me. Bless that kid's heart, he was trying to comfort me. He thought I was scared of Logan's jet-ski abilities and of falling again. If that were my only problem with Logan, life would be easy.

"Fine." I glared at Logan. He kicked his legs and effortlessly pulled me and my life jacket over to his jet-ski. He helped me get up and into position, handing me up the life jacket. I quickly put it on and waited for him to get up. A drop of blood spilled down my cheek and onto the bright orange fabric. I wondered if the resort was going to charge me to clean it.

Logan looked back to make sure I was ready and frowned. He bit the sleeve of his shirt and started to tear. With a sharp tug and a ripping sound, he removed the sleeve and handed it to me. "Here," he said. I stared at him for a moment until he added, "for your head."

"Thanks," I said grudgingly, pressing the dark fabric against the cut. He nodded and looked over at Tyler, who flashed him a weak grin and gave the thumbs-up signifying he was ready to go. Logan waited until Tyler was moving, and then carefully followed behind him.

I wrapped my arms around Logan's waist so I wouldn't be jostled off by the waves. Even through his life jacket, he was incredibly solid and warm beneath my palms. If he wasn't such a jerk, I would have enjoyed being this close to such a nice specimen of masculinity. My body was responding a little too nicely to being pressed up against him, and I had to stop myself from snuggling up further.

He's an ass, I reminded myself as my heartbeat started to race. *A muscled, handsome ass who is going to use this to his advantage.* I just knew once we got to shore that he would take all the glory for rescuing me.

CHAPTER SIX

Logan carefully followed Tyler to the dock where the attendant quickly took our keys and called the resort infirmary and told them to be expecting us. Logan lifted me from the seat to the dock, where my knees threatened to buckle as soon as I landed. He had his arm around me before I even had a chance to sag. I didn't want to, but I held onto his muscled arm. *Just for balance,* I told myself, *not because he's so nice to hold on to.*

Tyler came to my other side and wrapped my other arm over his shoulder. He was still too short for the action to work as intended, but it was such a sweet gesture, I didn't say anything. He puffed out his chest and helped carry me to the employee golf cart, even though it was Logan who was doing most of the work.

Together, the two of them got me settled as the jet-ski attendant hopped in the driver's seat and sped us all to the infirmary. It was only a short drive, but Tyler held onto me like I might go flying out of the cart at any moment. When we stopped, he made sure to help me inside as much as his small frame would allow. The nurse was waiting for us and quickly shuffled me off into an exam room as soon as we walked through the door.

"You two stay out here. I'll stay with her until the doctor comes in," she told a very worried-looking Tyler. "She'll be just fine. The room's too small for all of you to fit."

The exam room looked like every other doctor's office I had ever been to, only slightly smaller and decorated with stenciled seashells on the wall. The resort had a full-time doctor on staff as part of the resort package. I hadn't intended to use this service, but I was glad it was here.

The nurse took the now-soaked shirtsleeve and handed me some clean, white gauze to hold against the cut on my head as I sat down on the exam table. Now that some of the adrenaline was wearing off, the cut was starting to ache and throb, but at least I didn't appear to be bleeding anymore.

"Hello there," said a warm, baritone voice as the door opened. A tall, older gentleman with graying blonde hair walked into the room. He wore a resort polo but had on dark blue board shorts. He looked like he would be equally comfortable in a clinical setting or out surfing the waves. "I'm Dr. James."

"Olivia," I introduced myself. The nurse stepped out and closed the door behind her as the doctor shook my hand.

"The men outside say you fell off your jet-ski, hit your head, and were unconscious for at least two minutes." He leaned against the small counter, his eyes assessing my injuries and cataloging everything.

"That's what they tell me. I don't remember much." I did my best to smile, but my head was now pounding. I really just wanted to lay down and take a nap.

"How are you feeling?" Dr. James asked, turning to wash his hands in the sink.

"Stupid."

Dr. James chuckled as he reached for the paper towels. "Anything else? Any nausea, balance issues? Seeing spots?"

"I have a pretty terrible headache. When I first got out of the water, I was a little dizzy, but I feel better now." I sighed and looked up at him. "Other than the stupid and headache part."

"Good." Dr. James pulled out a penlight and shined it in my eyes. "Tell me your full name, age, and birthday."

"Olivia Michelle Statler. I'm twenty-seven and my birthday is October twenty-fifth." I blinked as he moved the light away. He proceeded to hit my knees with the strange triangle hammer from my childhood. Both knees popped up just as expected.

"Excellent. What is the current month? Date if you know it, but I know it's hard to keep track on vacation." Dr. James smiled as he put his hands on my neck and shoulders and checked for any injuries. Out of habit, I started to raise my wrist to check my watch for the date, but he caught my arm before I could see it.

"November. It's two weeks until Thanksgiving and a Tuesday, but that's all I got," I said with a rueful grin at my watch.

He released my arm and smiled. "You got me beat. I forgot Thanksgiving was coming up. Do you know where you are right now?"

"Island Oasis Resort, in the medical center." I knew these silly questions were just meant to check on my mental status, so I didn't mind answering the obvious. The idea that people often forgot this stuff after a head injury was rather sobering.

"Excellent. Follow my finger with your eyes and tell me what the last thing you remember is," the doctor said, holding one finger up and moving it from side to side.

"Turning on the engine to go see something Tyler was excited about. Then thinking, 'Oh crap!' as the wave hit. Then I was suddenly staring up at the sky."

There was a hole in my memory between the wave and the sky. I knew time had passed, but I couldn't remember even hitting the water. It was a little creepy to know I had been awake but had lost that memory.

"That's pretty normal in situations like these," Dr. James commented. He put on some gloves and reached for the cut on my head. I uncovered my injury and relaxed my arm as he took the gauze away and inspected the wound. "So, you're here as one of the travel agency promos, right?"

I started to nod, but my head was caught firmly in his hands. "Yeah."

"I hope this won't discourage you from recommending us," he said, releasing my head.

"Well, I certainly wasn't intending to test out your medical services, but it is nice knowing there is a full-time doctor on staff here." I glanced up toward the injury even though I knew I wouldn't be able to see it. It didn't hurt quite so much, but I was ready to kill for a couple of Tylenol.

Dr. James took off his gloves and rummaged around in a cabinet, his voice slightly muffled as he reached for something deep in its recesses. "It's the best pseudo-retirement I could think of. The hours are great, I get to surf, but I still get to practice."

"This place does seem pretty amazing," I replied. "Am I going to need stitches?"

"Nope. It looks like you were actually pretty lucky. You definitely have a concussion, but at least the cut on your head is fairly superficial. I'm just going to clean it up and you'll be good to go." He smiled and set out some supplies on the counter before putting on a clean pair of gloves.

"Really?" I looked down at the blood-soaked gauze in the trash. I thought that looked like a lot of blood.

"Head wounds tend to bleed a lot, but it's already stopped. The cut isn't deep enough to warrant stitches." He gently began cleaning the wound. "It's just under your hairline, but you probably won't even get a scar out of it."

"That's good," I said, wincing as he pressed down on the wound.

"I'll tell your admirers outside this as well, but no napping today. I also want someone to come and check on you a couple of times tonight and make sure you're able to wake up and answer questions." He pulled back and inspected his handiwork. "If you'd like, I can arrange it with the hotel staff."

"No naps? But I'm exhausted," I whined.

"You just smashed your brain hard enough to make you black out. We want to make sure that there isn't more damaged than we suspect. Another loss of consciousness would be very bad, and if you're napping, we'd miss it," he said sternly. "Also, I want you to take it easy for the next few days. No more jet-skiing this trip. And, unfortunately, no alcohol for a few days either. If your headache doesn't go away, gets worse, or you start feeling strange, come see me immediately."

"Okay," I answered. "I'll be good."

Dr. James smiled and patted my shoulder. "I'll give you a packet with all the instructions. It'll have all the things you need to do, like see your regular doctor when you get home, and warning signs and such."

I nodded and he gave me his hand to help me off the exam table. Together, we headed out to the waiting room. Logan and Tyler both stood as we came out. The nurse handed Dr. James a printed sheet of instructions which he then gave me.

"She's good to go, guys. Keep an eye on her, though. Don't let her nap today and she'll need someone to check on her tonight," Dr. James told my visitors.

"Yes, sir," Tyler said quickly. He had some color back in his face and a soda in his hand. By the way he was making sure I stayed close to him, though, he was going to be a little protective of me for a while. I loved that he was concerned and that I now had a pint-sized protector.

"Not a problem, doctor. I'll make sure she's woken up myself," Logan said, shaking the doctor's hand.

"No, you won't," I said vehemently. There was no way Logan Hayes would be coming in my bedroom to wake me up during the night. There was no way he was getting in my bedroom again, period. The doctor's eyebrows went up into his hair as he looked back and forth between us.

"What I mean is," I explained, trying to keep calm. The doctor didn't need to know about my hatred for the man who apparently saved me. "I'll have the hotel staff do it. No reason for you to lose sleep."

"As you wish," Logan conceded. He flashed me his most charming smile, one that said he thought he was going to change my mind. I nearly smacked him. If the doctor and nurse hadn't been looking at us like I might be crazy, I would have.

"Thank you, Dr. James," I said, turning to shake his hand a final time. "I appreciate your help. I should go get ready for dinner."

His grip was strong on mine as his eyebrows returned to their rightful places on his face. "Keep that cut clean and come see me if you have any questions."

"I will. Thank you." I put my hand on Tyler's shoulder and nudged him toward the door. He smiled back at the doctor, and the two of us headed out the door with Logan trailing right behind.

◈

CHAPTER SEVEN

The three of us walked quietly along the manicured path back to the main building. The wind had picked up, but it was still warm as the sun prepared to dip her toes into the ocean below. I couldn't believe the day was almost over. With all the excitement, I had completely lost track of time.

"Are you going to the welcome banquet tonight?" Logan asked as we rounded one of the resort pools. No one was swimming, but the water rippled gently in the breeze as we passed.

"Yes," I replied hesitantly. I had already planned on going with Tyler and Maddy, but the idea of him being there made me a little queasy. Despite all Logan's help today, I still didn't trust him. Once burned, twice shy. I wasn't about to let him ruin me again, even if he did save me from drowning.

"I'll see you there, then," he said with a grin. "Take care of her, Tyler."

Tyler nodded, tightening his grip around my arm, which was still draped over his shoulder, even though I was perfectly capable of walking on my own. "You got it. See you tonight, Logan."

Logan's smile softened as he turned to walk down a separate path. His shirt was still missing the sleeve, but he strutted like he was wearing a tuxedo. I wished he wasn't so damn attractive. I didn't want to keep looking at him, but my eyes wouldn't leave his form. When he finally turned the corner, I shook my head, trying to clear the image of him from my mind.

"Tyler?" I pulled my arm away and turned so that we were facing one another. He was no longer pale, but he still looked shaken by the day's events. I felt horribly for having scared him so badly. "I really want to thank you. You saved my life."

I was expecting him to blush or shrug, but instead he bit his cheek and looked down at the ground. He looked like he had a terrible secret.

"What's wrong?" I asked, putting my hands on his shoulders. He fidgeted slightly, but didn't attempt to escape.

"I didn't save you. Logan did." He dug the toe of his shoe into a small pile of sand, refusing to look up at me.

"What do you mean? Logan said you were the hero." I squeezed his shoulders slightly and waited as he deepened the hole with his foot. He took a slow breath before he spoke.

"When I saw you fall, I swam over to you as fast

as I could, screaming the whole way." He looked up tentatively at me, his big brown eyes unsure of what I was going to think of him. "I got to you first, but with my life jacket and the waves, I could barely hold onto you. I was able to get your head above the water, but you would have drowned if Logan hadn't shown up."

"So, Logan was the one who got me to calmer waters?" I asked, keeping my voice gentle.

Tyler nodded, his face crumpling. "I didn't even get the jet-ski and your life jacket until he told me to. I didn't know what to do. You weren't moving. All I could think was that you were dead."

I pulled him to me in a hug, and his skinny arms wrapped around my waist in reciprocation as he buried his face in my shoulder. I held him tightly, smoothing the hair on the back of his head. I could feel his fear and shame vibrating through him. He thought he had somehow failed me.

The idea that Logan would forfeit the glory to a skinny teenager baffled me. The Logan Hayes I knew loved the spotlight. He relished being the golden boy who could do no wrong. If reporters were here, he would have posed for pictures and signed autographs as "Logan Hayes: Hero." But, according to Tyler's story, he hadn't done that. He had given Tyler all the credit and accepted a supporting role. I was sure there had to be a trick behind it.

"Tyler," I said quietly. He sniffled and pulled his face out of my shoulder to look at me. I smiled down at him. "Tyler, if you hadn't been there, I would have drowned regardless of Logan's intervention. If he's giving you the credit, then you deserve it. I owe you a lot. If Logan says you saved me, then you saved me. He wouldn't lie about something like that. The man likes his spotlight too much."

Tyler frowned. "But Aunt Liv, I really didn't do anything special."

"I think you did. You are my hero, Tyler. I'm very proud of you."

Tyler thought for a moment, and his frown slowly morphed into a bashful smile. "I'm glad you're okay, Aunt Liv."

"Me too," I said, giving him one last squeeze before releasing him. "Now, let's get you back to your mom."

"You sure you want to do that? You know she's going to be furious with you," Tyler told me, positioning my arm over his shoulder again. "I can't save you from her."

I laughed. "It will be painful. But, I'd rather get her lecture on life jacket safety over with before we go to dinner."

"The trick is to say you're sorry. A lot. And give her hugs. Whenever she gets mad, it's really just because she's actually worried," Tyler said knowingly. I stopped short and he turned to look up at me.

"You are a smart kid, you know that?"

He shrugged. "Nah, I just know my mom."

CHAPTER EIGHT

I checked my hair in the mirror one last time before opening the door to leave. My injury was barely visible, but I was surprised my ears weren't still red from the lecture Maddy had given me. She delivered a talking to that would have made my own mother pat her on the back for a job well done.

I had followed Tyler's advice and apologized profusely, promising never to take my life jacket off again, and then hugged her. She had stared at me for a moment before hugging me back like I had just been resurrected from the dead, but that was the end of the lecture.

Smoothing one last flyaway strand of dirty-blonde hair up into my loose bun, I felt pleased with my overall appearance. I wore a light blue chiffon dress with a sparkly rhinestone belt that hid a multitude of sins but still showed my curves. It was casual and

elegant at the same time. Maddy had suggested that I put my hair up with this dress, and I had to admit that with the addition of some dangling earrings, I looked pretty darn good.

I gave one last photographer-ready smile to the mirror, opened the door, and promptly smacked into a wall of solid muscle in a suit.

"I'm so sorry," I apologized as I backed away from the figure I had just run into. "I didn't see you there."

"No problem at all, Olivia," Logan said warmly. I felt my cheeks heat instantly. Of all the people to crash into, I had to crash into him. This was just not my day. With an appreciative eye, he ogled me up and down, making me want to hit him upside the head. "You are stunning."

"Thank you," I huffed, simultaneously enjoying and resenting the compliment. "You look nice yourself."

If anyone looked amazing, it was Logan. The playboy billionaire knew how to dress. He wore a dark suit with strong lines that accented his broad shoulders and muscular build. His usually messy hair was combed neatly back, making his jaw appear strong and chiseled. His friendly brown eyes were warmly set in a smiling, suntanned face. The only thing that kept him from airbrushed GQ magazine perfection was the red sunburn across the bridge of his nose.

"Blue is wonderful on you," he mused, reminding me that he was watching. The thought sent warmth through my core, which just made me blush harder. The last thing I wanted was any sort of

47

attraction to a man like him. He was a snake in a very good-looking suit.

"Thank you." I smoothed the front of my dress, suddenly feeling self-conscious under his intense gaze. The corners of his eyes crinkled with amusement at my discomfort, which only further raised my temperature. He had to know the effect he had on women-- even women who were actively trying not to be flustered by him. "I was just on my way to go get Tyler. I take it you're staying at the resort as well?"

"I am. I was invited here just like you were." He stood tall, unconsciously holding a handsome pose. I wished he wasn't so damn easy on the eyes. I couldn't stop looking at him in that suit and thinking of what was underneath it.

"I would think a billionaire playboy wouldn't need to take free vacations," I said, hoping he couldn't see the effect his suit was having on me. His shoulders were just so deliciously broad and tapered down to a tight V that made me ache for his masculine touch. It just wasn't fair that he was so gorgeous and evil at the same time.

He shrugged, drawing my attention back up to his muscular shoulders. "I do actually look into places that my company promotes from time to time."

"And the fact that the owner just happens to be one of your good college buddies certainly doesn't hurt either, I suppose." I smoothed my hair back again and resumed my walk to the elevators. Logan fell into step beside me.

"You mean Noah Black?" He asked as we faced the silver elevator doors and waited for them to

arrive. The stairs were available, but after the day's events, I didn't want to risk them in heels. Unfortunately, that meant I had to stand there and wait with Logan.

"As if there were another Noah Black?" I wished the elevator would hurry up. The door chimed softly, and I dashed inside. Logan hit the lobby button, but I hit the floor below us.

"Noah is always happy to help me with my travel arrangements. I certainly bring him enough business." Logan definitely did give Noah Black and his hotel company, Diamond Hotels, enough business. Diamond Hotels was the preferred provider on Travel, Inc.'s website. The two men had made each other very rich.

The elevator rang as we reached the second floor. I quickly stepped out. I was about to let him continue on down to the lobby, but there was something I needed to know first. I turned and thrust my arm out to hold the door open.

"Did you or Tyler save me?" I asked, watching his face intently.

"Tyler," he answered without hesitation. I couldn't detect any hints of deception in his face, but then again, I knew he was an expert liar. Especially when it came to me.

"That's not what he said." The elevator chirped for the doors to close, but I kept them open. Logan looked thoughtful for a moment before answering.

"Tyler wasn't strong enough to keep you above the surface by himself. The waves were rough. I helped. He deserves the praise, though, not me." Logan took

a step closer to me but still within the confines of the elevator. "Tyler was the hero, and I'll stand by that."

With that, he gently pushed my arm out of the way so the doors would close, and he continued down toward the lobby without me. I stared at my open-mouthed reflection in the shiny metal door. Tyler had said as much, but Logan's lack of desire for praise made no sense. He was the type of person who relished these kinds of opportunities, and carrying the hero's mantle seemed like something he would enjoy.

"Aunt Liv!" Tyler called out, yanking me from my thoughts. He hurried toward me as I turned from the elevator to see him and Maddy coming down the hallway. Tyler looked uncomfortable in his dress shirt and crisp pants; he was all awkward limbs and gawky angles that made the clothes look too small and too large at the same time. His nose and mouth were too big for his face, and his light brown hair was falling in his eyes.

He was totally geeky and graceless right now, but there was a handsome promise underneath his awkwardness. But, as he tripped on his oversized feet down the hallway, he was just a pre-teen boy with no grace. He was stuck being the ugly duckling for right now.

Perhaps that's what Logan saw, and that was why he was giving him this moment of glory. There weren't exactly a lot of paparazzi on the island. The media gain from this would be small without pictures, but making Tyler feel important would be huge. It was common knowledge that I considered him a part of my family and that he was Maddy's world. Perhaps

Logan was going to use this as some sort of bargaining maneuver.

"You look really pretty, Aunt Liv," Tyler said once he got to me. His hair was gelled and messy in an apparent attempt to mimic Logan's easy bed-head look. Unfortunately, without Logan's team of hairdresser's, it wasn't having quite the same effect. He still looked cute, though.

"You look very handsome yourself," I complimented him. He grinned and stood up a little taller.

"What about me?" Maddy asked, finally catching up to her son. She wore a long, dark blue halter dress that hung in beautiful swoops. Maddy was curvy, and this dress hugged her in all the right places. She was always joking that she was trying to lose Tyler's baby weight and that it would come off any month now. The dress was perfect on her, and it even managed to disguise her walking boot.

"Red-carpet-ready!" I told her as she struck a model pose.

"You're always pretty, Mom," Tyler praised. She grinned at him and then kissed his cheek.

"You're just trying to get me on your good side," she teased, but I knew she treasured his compliment. She turned to me and gave me a once over. "How are you feeling?"

"For the millionth time, I'm fine, *Mom*." I rolled my eyes. She frowned and took my chin in her hand so she could look closer at the cut on my head. It didn't even hurt anymore. "Seriously, Maddy, I'm fine. Tyler did a great job of rescuing me, and the doctor says I'm going to live."

Maddy frowned as she let me go, but as she looked at Tyler, the frown transitioned to a proud smile. He looked back and forth between the two of us and then rolled his eyes. He hit the button for the elevator, which arrived more quickly this time.

Tyler held his mother's arm, providing the support she needed with her walking boot as we came out into the lobby. She was a good six inches shorter than I was, so he was much more supportive for her than he was for me after the jet-ski accident. He looked incredibly pleased with himself as we stepped out of the building and into the night air. We walked quietly for a moment, enjoying the warm, tropical evening.

"This has been a much needed vacation," she said, giving Tyler a gentle squeeze.

"You deserve it," I told her. "You're the main reason we're able to be here. I never could have done this without you. The business never would have gotten off the ground without you."

"Keep stroking my ego," she said with a grin as we walked down the path to the main dining restaurant. "And I might forget your sins today."

CHAPTER NINE

The weather report said a storm was supposed to be moving in on the island the next day, but the sky above us was cloudless and full of stars. A gentle breeze, warm and moist, danced through the greenery, ruffled the pools and ponds, and then caressed our skin like the fingertips of a lover as we walked from the main building to the dining hall. It was exactly what a tropical paradise should be.

The resort boasted four restaurants, but this meet and greet banquet was being held in the main dining area. The only guests at the resort were travel agency representatives, so it was supposed to be just a laid-back, fun little get together. Since the resort wasn't officially open, and it was still technically the off season, we had the place to ourselves.

From a distance, the dining facility seemed to be made of windows and light. Music spilled out into the quiet night as the elegant silhouettes of the guests floated across the windows. I wondered how many people were here. I knew there was my agency, and also Travel, Inc., and at least three other agencies were on the island. Even with that in mind, the party looked small.

Tyler opened the door and held it open like a gentleman for his mother and me. He looked excited to be invited to an adult event, and I hoped it was going to live up to his expectations.

The room was large and spacious with a small buffet table in the center. I could see platters of chocolate strawberries, fresh fruit, finger sandwiches, cheese and crackers, and even what looked like fresh sushi. The room had ample seating but was also very spacious. There was plenty of room to move around and converse with the other guests. The windows facing the ocean were open to catch the sea breeze and let in the sound of the ocean.

An elegant woman with strawberry blonde hair was walking toward the three of us with a big smile across her face. A tall man with dark hair trailed behind her, stopping to pop a strawberry in his mouth before catching up.

"You must be Olivia Statler," the woman greeted me, extending her hand. I shook it, surprised to find it strong and calloused.

"Yes, and you must be Isabel Black," I replied. I had heard that the wife of the hotel magnate, Noah Black, still worked daily with sharks. Her strong grip and suntanned skin pretty much confirmed that. I was slightly surprised. I figured that anyone who married into billions would relax into a life of leisure, but from what I had heard, she had actually increased the extent of her research.

"Izzy, please. Isabel is only for when I'm in trouble." She grinned as she released my hand and went to shake Maddy's next. "You must be Madison, and that makes you...Tyler."

Izzy extended her hand to shake Tyler's. He hesitated for only a second before enthusiastically shaking her hand. "I'm very pleased to make your acquaintance," he said formally.

"Likewise," Izzy told him. He grinned up at her, forgetting to let go of her hand and still shaking it. Izzy looked over at Maddy and giggled. She didn't pull her hand away, though.

"It looks like I might have some competition," the tall man said, coming up behind Izzy. Tyler suddenly realized what he was doing and turned a deep shade of crimson before finally letting go of Izzy's hand.

"This is my husband, Noah," Izzy introduced. Noah shook everyone's hands, including Tyler's. Tyler did not hold onto his.

"It's a pleasure to finally meet you. I do a lot of business with several of your resorts," I told him.

"And I appreciate that," Noah said. He wrapped his arm around Izzy's shoulders and smiled warmly. He had the most amazing blue eyes, but they only sparkled when he looked at Izzy. Love seemed to float around the two of them like a happy cloud. "We're so glad you all could make it. The resort is officially opening in time for the Christmas season, but we were hoping to generate some positive buzz beforehand. What do you think so far?"

"It's amazing," Tyler blurted out, his ears reddening when everyone turned to look at him.

"Anything in particular that's awesome?" Noah asked. "You are among one of our key demographics, after all. I'd love to know what you think."

Tyler swallowed hard but stood up taller. I knew he was a shy kid, so talking to strangers wasn't easy for him. He was doing great. "The food. Plus the game room is sweet."

Noah grinned. "You like the pinball machine?"

"The comic book one? It's the coolest one I've ever seen," he answered honestly. He was still blushing, but he sounded a little more sure of himself.

"Excellent!" Noah made a fist-pumping motion that made Izzy roll her eyes. "I picked it out specifically for that room. *Someone* wanted to go with an island-themed one. See? I was right."

Izzy rolled her eyes again but smiled at Tyler. "Now he's never going to let me live that one down." Noah laughed and kissed her cheek, making her smile.

I felt the breeze of the door opening behind me and turned to see Logan and his bodyguard walk in. The bodyguard melted into the shadows as Logan joined our small circle. I tried not to shy away when he decided to stand next to me, but it was hard to be so close to him.

"I see you've met our local hero," Logan said, gesturing to Tyler. I didn't know it was possible, but Tyler's blush blushed. If he turned any redder, he wouldn't have any blood left in his body.

"Hero?" Izzy asked, frowning slightly and looking

quickly between Logan and Tyler.

Logan nodded. "Tyler saved Olivia from drowning in the ocean earlier this afternoon."

"Oh my gosh," Izzy exclaimed, her hand going to her mouth and wide eyes going to mine. "Are you okay?"

"I have a slight concussion, but the doctor says I'll be fine," I told her. "Tyler did a good job."

"You must be very brave, Tyler." Izzy put her hand on Tyler's shoulder and he stood a little taller. "What happened?"

Tyler's blush must have gone all the way down to his toes. He looked up at Logan, a little lost as to what he was supposed to say. I knew he didn't feel like he was the hero. "Um, well..."

"Olivia and Tyler were jet-skiing over by the reef," Logan explained, his voice low and dramatic. Tyler gave him a grateful nod as he continued their story. "Tyler was in the water and Olivia was coming to get him when she hit a wave and was thrown from her jet-ski. She was knocked unconscious and was drowning. Tyler not only swam to her rescue, but kept her above the water. He kept calm the whole time."

"You helped a lot too, Mr. Hayes," Tyler said quietly.

Logan shrugged, deflecting any of the credit. "I just happened to be nearby. I didn't do anything special. You were the one who really saved her."

Tyler peeked around shyly at the group of adults, waiting to see their reactions.

"That is amazing!" Izzy exclaimed. The other

adults murmured in agreement and Tyler beamed. Every adult was beholding at him with awe and he knew it. His chest puffed out a little bit, and he stood up a little straighter as his confidence soared.

Bless Logan for giving him this moment. I had been sure that once we were in a public setting he would take all the credit for my rescue, but instead he had given it all to Tyler. I could barely believe it; the man did have a shred of decency in him, but this was the most generous thing he could have done for Tyler. Seeing the confidence in Tyler's face, I could almost imagine that Logan wasn't evil.

"I think this calls for a toast," Noah said, motioning to the bartender in the corner. The bartender quickly hurried over carrying a tray with six champagne flutes. He handed a specific one to Tyler.

"This one is sparkling cider," the bartender explained to Maddy as she reached out to take it before Tyler could.

"Could I get a cider, too? I'm not supposed to have anything alcoholic today," I asked the bartender with a blush. He nodded, and once his tray had only the one champagne glass, hurried back to the bar to return with one filled with cider.

"To Tyler, the hero of the island," Logan announced once I had my glass.

"To Tyler," everyone echoed, raising their glasses. Tyler's grin threatened to split his face in half. This certainly was a vacation that he was never going to forget.

As we sipped our champagne, a man in a white uniform and chef hat stepped into the center of the room. "Dinner is served," he announced.

Two tables rolled in behind him and were added to the buffet table in the middle. From where I was standing, I could see roast beef, lobster, crab legs, and more. There was enough food to feed an army.

"Will you sit next to me?" Izzy asked Tyler as we headed toward the food. He looked to his mother's smile and then nodded enthusiastically. He was crushing hard on her.

"That is a lot of food," I commented to Noah as we joined the other guests lining up for the food. We were the last two in line. There were only maybe fifteen people, but there was enough food for double, if not triple, that many guests on the table.

"We were expecting more people to be here, but the threat of a hurricane scared several groups away," he explained, picking up a plate.

"Hurricane? Last I heard it was just a tropical storm, and much farther North," I said with a frown. Technically, it was still hurricane season in the Caribbean, but the odds of a hurricane actually happening were incredibly low. It was the reason we had been willing to risk the trip.

"It was upgraded to a tropical storm this evening, but the word 'hurricane' was said somewhere, and now it's all people are talking about." Noah shook his head as he piled crab legs onto his plate. "Don't worry, though. The island is safe. A hurricane hasn't hit these shores in over twenty years, and even then the damage was minimal."

"That's good to know." I piled mashed potatoes onto my plate. I hadn't realized how hungry I was until I saw the food.

"But just in case you were wondering, the hotel is still hurricane-ready," Noah informed me. "Each building is secure and there are a series of tunnels that connect the two main buildings and several other areas of the resort. If a hurricane ever did hit the island, the resort is very safe and very ready. And all ecologically friendly, of course."

I paused from putting a lobster claw on my plate and looked at him. "If I didn't know better, I might think you were trying to sell me something, Noah."

He laughed and handed me a napkin from the end of the table. "It's hard to turn off the sales pitch sometimes. I'm very proud of this resort."

"As you should be. It's beautiful, and the fact that it's all green-certified is amazing," I told him as we headed to a round table. Izzy, Tyler, Maddy, and Logan were already sitting, all of them digging into their food with a passion. Noah took the seat on the other side of Izzy, leaving me to sit next to Logan. I wished there was just one more seat at the table so I didn't have to be so close.

"Will you and Izzy be staying here this week as well?" I asked Noah once we had slowed down on shoving the delicious food into our faces enough to talk. If they continued to feed us this well, I was going to go home ten pounds heavier. Even with that image in my head, I was tempted to go back for more. It was just that good. Logan stood and went back to the buffet table. Apparently he didn't care about the weight either.

"No," Noah said, shaking his head sadly. "Our jet

is actually being prepped now. We have to be in New York by tomorrow morning."

"That's too bad. It look's like Tyler's really enjoying Izzy." I nodded my head across the table where it appeared the two of them were having an animated discussion about something. I thought I heard the word "shark," but I wasn't sure. Whatever it was, Tyler looked like he was having the time of his life. Noah smiled at the two of them, his eyes soft. Izzy looked up and caught his gaze, her eyes twinkling at him before returning to her conversation.

An old-fashioned phone ring came from inside Noah's suit jacket. He pulled it out and frowned at the screen. "I'm terribly sorry, I need to take this. Excuse me."

He stood and put the phone to his ear as he stepped toward the rear of the building. I sat quietly watching Tyler and Izzy interact until Logan returned. He had the lobster claw I was thinking of getting. I decided that I didn't actually need it and instead stood up to get a drink from the bar. I was sure the bartender could make me a virgin-something.

"How's your head?" he asked, cracking open the shell. I winced at the sound, especially combined with the mention of my head.

"It doesn't hurt anymore, but I'm definitely tired. Exhausted, really. I'm going to go get a drink." I hoped he'd take the hint that I wasn't up for conversation.

"I'll come with you," he said, pushing away his plate and standing. I turned and hurried to the bar. I wished he would just leave me alone. I heard him follow behind me, and it took all my strength not to sigh.

"Virgin strawberry daiquiri, please," I requested once I reached the ornate wooden counter. The bartender quickly started mixing ingredients.

"One for me too, if you don't mind," Logan chimed in. The bartender nodded and added more juice to his blender.

"You know there's no alcohol in this, right?" I asked, crossing my arms against the countertop.

"I happen to be a fan of virgin strawberry daiquiris." He leaned back against the bar, looking completely at ease. His jacket hung open, and I could see the definition of his muscles under his thin white dress shirt. Damn him for looking good without even trying. It messed with my head that he could look like an angel but be such a devil.

He continued to talk. "I always thought it was a cruel joke that after all the excitement of a concussion that you aren't allowed to nap." The bartender handed us our drinks and he took a big sip before continuing. I really wished that the daiquiri had alcohol. It would make this situation so much more bearable.

"Is that so?" I glanced around the room to see if I could escape, but Noah was still on the phone, Tyler and Izzy were deep in conversation, and Maddy was busy talking with one of the other guests. No easy outs.

"With all the adrenaline and movement that comes with an accident, it's only natural to want to sleep after," he continued. "If it was your ankle instead of your head, no one would think twice about letting you pass out and recover. But, since it's the head, no nap. So, not only are you exhausted and injured, you have people poking you and telling you not to sleep."

"You sound like you've had this happen to you once or twice," I replied before realizing I was engaging him in conversation. Now I *had* to talk to him.

"I used to play football. Even played in college. Plus, having an older brother kind of predisposes kids to injuries," he said with a laugh.

Football certainly explained his broad-shouldered physique. He was easy to imagine out on a field in pads and a jersey, and I found my body responding favorably to the image. I really wished he wasn't such a jerk, because there were things I would enjoy doing to that body.

"What position did you play?" I asked, taking another sip of my drink and trying not to think of what he looked like without his shirt on.

"Usually wide receiver, though sometimes I'd play tight end." He smiled his movie star smile at me and I couldn't look away. I wished I didn't find him so damn attractive. I hated him and what he did to me, but one flash of that mega-watt grin and my knees went to putty. It wasn't fair. My body and my mind definitely had very different opinions of the man.

"Were you any good?"

"Not really," he said, shaking his head. "I tell people I played in college, but it was mostly on the bench. I have a feeling dad helped get me on the team. I loved the game, but I don't have much natural talent for it."

"Logan Hayes admitting that he's not good at something?" I turned and exaggerated looking out the nearest window. "I don't see any pigs with wings out there..."

"It's dark out, and they tend to fly higher up in the atmosphere," he replied. "Don't tell anyone, though. Could ruin my football reputation."

I laughed, and was surprised to find it was genuine. I could barely believe I was enjoying his company, and not just because of his looks. He was being wonderful and sweet--not only me, but Tyler. I took a sip of my drink and wondered if I hit my head harder than I thought. I had sworn I would stay away from him.

"What about you? Anything you aren't good at?" Logan asked. His brown eyes focused on me, absorbing my every detail as if it were terribly important, and it made my heart speed up. I hadn't had a man look at me like that in a very long time...since the last time he had looked at me like that, in fact.

"Jet-skiing," I answered with a straight face. His laugh filled the room and I grinned. "Actually, I want to thank you again. You were great with Tyler."

"He's a good kid. He actually reminds me a lot of myself when I was his age." His eyes went distant as he remembered his own gawky years. I tried to think of him as a scared, skinny boy and couldn't reconcile the image. He oozed too much charm and self-assurance for me to see him as anything but the man before me.

"I really do appreciate it. You didn't have to stay with him while I was with the doctor, but I'm really grateful that you did," I said. I hoped he knew how sincere I was. Despite my dislike for him and his business tactics, he had done the right thing that afternoon. "Thank you for all your help today."

"It was no trouble. I wasn't going to just abandon the kid." He took a sip of his drink and shrugged like heroics were an everyday occurrence for him. "I'm just glad you're okay."

A genuine smile etched its way onto my face. Maybe I had misjudged him. Maybe he had changed from the sneaky conman who had almost ruined my business and broken my heart. I wasn't quite ready to trust him completely. But today he had not only saved my life, but also made someone who I cared about very happy. I glanced over at Tyler. Izzy was busy telling two men from another travel agency of Tyler's heroics. Tyler was smiling and basking in the attention. I hadn't seen that side of him since before the move. That alone was worth giving Logan another chance.

"Thank you." I smiled and really meant it.

"And besides, if I had let you drown, I wouldn't be able to have your company become part of Travel, Inc.," Logan added. "Maybe you can give us a 'saved your life' discount."

I felt the smile slide off my face just as quickly as it had found its way there. It was all just a business maneuver. He hadn't changed. He was just leading me on. Again. The charming man was just an act. He was only interested in acquiring my business. I should have known better than to let my guard down, even for an instant.

"If you think that today is going to have any bearing on our business negotiations, you are sorely mistaken, Mr. Hayes" I said coldly. I couldn't believe his nerve. "It will be a cold day in hell before I sell my company to you. You had your chance two years ago and you blew it."

"Olivia, I didn't mean-"

"Now, if you'll excuse me, I have things to do," I said, cutting him off. I set my drink down with a loud thunk. All the warm, fuzzy feelings I had toward him were gone. He was willing to use the fact that he rescued me as a business tactic. He was willing to use Tyler as a business tactic. That was not acceptable to me.

I stalked over to the table where Tyler and Izzy were chatting. Maddy had joined them as well, and I flung myself into the chair next to her. From the corner of my eye, I could see Logan sag against the bar, frustration painted on his face. He knew he had just screwed himself, and that gave me a little bubble of smug pride. I knew the real Logan Hayes.

"What did the eel look like?" Izzy asked Tyler. They were apparently discussing the marine life he had seen earlier that afternoon and were oblivious to everything else in the room.

"It had black and white spots," Tyler answered, his face furrowed in concentration. "Little ones."

"That was a Spotted Moray Eel, then," Izzy told him. "What else did you see?"

Tyler thought for a moment as Noah came up

behind Izzy. He put his hands on her shoulders, and she turned to look up at him. Her face was full of trust and pure happiness at his touch. It was hard not to be a little envious of how much their love shone through in just a simple touch. They were lucky.

"I'm really sorry, Izzy," Noah interrupted, "but we need to be going. The plane's ready and the pilot's anxious to leave."

Izzy stood gracefully. "Tyler, it was wonderful to meet you. Madison and Olivia, thank you so much for coming. I hope you have a wonderful rest of your trip."

"Thank you so much for inviting us," I replied. "From what I've seen so far, I'll be recommending this resort to my clients."

"That's exactly what we want to hear," Noah said with a grin. "It was wonderful to meet you all."

Izzy gave Tyler a hug as Noah pushed her chair in for her. Tyler turned a delightful shade of red at her touch. He *definitely* had a little crush on Izzy. He smiled absentmindedly after her as she and Noah headed to the door.

Logan met the couple at the door and gave them both hugs. I had read that Noah and Logan had met in school and formed a fast friendship. I certainly believed it, especially as Logan's travel company had some exclusive perks with Diamond Hotels that no one else seemed to have. I wondered if Noah knew just how much Logan was using him for those perks.

My jaw creaked as I let out the biggest yawn of my life. I hadn't realized just how tired I was. Between the accident and the stress of the day, I was exhausted.

"I'm going to head to bed, Maddy," I said, rising to my feet. "It's been a long day."

"All right. Do you need me to come check on you tonight?" she asked. She was such a mom, and I loved her for it.

"No, I've got it covered," I answered. I went and gave Maddy a hug over the back of the chair. "The front desk is going to call, and if I don't pick up or answer their questions appropriately, they will come into the room to check on me."

Maddy considered my answer for a moment and nodded. "Okay. If you need anything, you let me know."

"I always do," I said with a smile. "Breakfast tomorrow?"

"Sounds good to me," she replied. Tyler nodded in agreement. "Have a good night."

I went over and gave Tyler a hug. "Thank you again for saving me today. You were awesome," I whispered.

"Anytime, Aunt Liv," he whispered back. He gave me a quick squeeze before remembering a question. "Izzy was telling me about some of the fish that live around here. You want to go snorkeling with me and mom tomorrow? No jet ski required."

"You got it, kid," I said with a wink. He grinned. "I'll see you in the morning."

I collected my things and headed to the door. Logan opened it for me as I reached for it. Instead of walking through it, I reached for the other side and helped myself. I didn't want even that much from him.

"I'm sorry about bringing business up. I know this is your vacation and-"

"Just drop it, okay?" I snapped, cutting him off. I took a deep breath and attempted to use a more even voice. "Thank you for your help today, but please, leave me alone."

With that I walked out into the night, leaving him holding the unused door. The wind was picking up from across the waves and whipped my skirt around my ankles, threatening to trip me. The last thing I wanted was for Logan to see me trip and come help me. Again.

I pulled up on the fabric and held onto it to keep it tamed while I walked. Without thinking, I glanced back at the brightly-lit building, assuming he must have gone back to the party. Instead, he stood there, still holding the door against the wind and watching me fade into the night.

CHAPTER TEN

The sky was solid gray. There were no individual clouds; it was just a jelled block of achromatic gray. As we walked along the ocean's edge, the water seemed strangely calm as it lapped against the sandy beach. It was almost as if the sea was expending its energy elsewhere. It seemed possible, as according to the resort's weather report the storm was still safely north and supposed to miss the entire island completely.

Up ahead, I could see a boy playing fetch with a dog, the two of them bounding through the waves and spraying water under their feet. The boy looked familiar, and as I came closer, I realized it was Tyler. I hadn't seen him since breakfast, where we had decided that neither one of us was really interested in snorkeling with the sky so dark. Without the sunshine, the colors of the fish and coral would be muted and dull. There were plenty of other things that we each wanted to do more than look at gray fish.

"Tyler?" I called out to the boy as I came closer. When his head whipped around, there was a big grin plastered on his face. He called the dog and the two of them came sprinting over, sand and water flying from their feet.

"Aunt Liv!" he greeted me, stopping just inches before giving me a hug as he realized he was soaking wet. The canine sniffed excitedly at my feet, its long, thin tail wagging at a furious pace.

"Whose dog is this?" It looked like the one from yesterday before jet-skiing. I held out my hand, expecting the pooch to smell it, but instead a warm, wet tongue kissed it.

"Spock," Tyler stated. He pet the dog's head and Spock wiggled with happiness. "Dr. James said he's a local stray, but that's it's fine if I play with him."

"Does your mom know you're playing with a stray?" I asked.

"She's busy with a pottery class." He threw a stick and Spock bounded gleefully after it. I raised my eyebrows and put my hands on my hips. He hadn't answered my question. Tyler sighed. "No. But Dr. James says he is really nice. He's really smart, too."

I gave the dog a skeptical look. It had just returned, but with a different stick than the one Tyler had thrown. The dog was pure mutt. There might have been some sort of lab in his genetic history, but the individual breeds had become so mixed it was impossible to tell what heritage the dog could claim. I had to admit that his floppy ears and doggy grin were rather adorable.

"Spock, sit," Tyler commanded. The dog promptly dropped to a sitting position, his tail still wagging furiously. Tyler grinned at me. "Spock, speak."

Spock yipped, dropping the stick in the process. Tyler dropped to his knees and began rubbing the dog's body and showering him with praise. Spock's ribs were even more clearly visible today, as well as several other signs of hunger and lack of attention.

"Did you teach him that?" I asked. I reached out to scratch Spock's ears and was rewarded with a doggy moan of pleasure that made me giggle.

"Yeah. He's really good," Tyler said. He smiled with just a hint of sadness at the mutt. "I can't believe nobody on the island wants him."

I wanted to hug Tyler close to ease the sudden ache in my heart. I knew he was really struggling with the abandonment by his father. The two had been close before his dad decided to run off with one of his clients and leave everything behind. Unfortunately, the new love interest didn't like kids, and so Tyler's dad had pretty much disowned him. It hurt Tyler far more than he let on.

"What else have you taught him?" I asked, changing the subject. Tyler's eyes lit up again.

"He can come, and we're working on rolling-over, but he keeps getting distracted." Tyler threw the stick again and Spock barked joyfully as he chased it. I watched as the dog picked up the discarded stick and then sprinted proudly back to his new best friend.

"Come here, Spock," I called, patting my leg. To my surprise, he came and snuggled his mangy head into my leg. Maddy was going to be thrilled. She wasn't a dog person, but there was no way Tyler was going to give up this mutt. I could feel the tension of future drama building as I saw the love in Tyler's eyes when he looked at Spock.

"He likes you, Aunt Liv." Tyler grinned at me. I peered down at the very cuddly puppy and sighed. I was going to be helping Tyler convince his mom that the dog was a good idea. I never could say no to a big pair of brown eyes.

"Give me the stick, Spock," I commanded. The dog quickly dropped it at my feet and stood waiting with bated breath for me to throw it. I tossed it into the waves and he bounded off to fetch it. "How long have you been out here with him, Tyler?"

"Since breakfast." Tyler's eyes followed the dog, and he grinned as Spock sprinted back to drop the stick at our feet. "I met him yesterday by the storage shed at the dock. Dr. James says he likes to hide there. I brought him some of my breakfast because he looked hungry yesterday."

The thin ribs suggested that the dog looked hungry every day. "I see why he likes you so much, then."

"It's not just the food, Aunt Liv." Tyler looked at me with solemn eyes. "I think he's lonely. The other dogs ignore him. We're a lot alike."

The simple truth in his statement broke my heart. Tyler saw himself in this mutt.

"Seems like you two were made for each other, then," I said softly. I made a mental note to look into how to bring a dog back to the United States. If I took care of that part, Spock stood a fighting chance at convincing Maddy.

"Yup." Tyler looked up at me and smiled, then waved to someone coming down the beach behind me. "Hi, Logan!"

I closed my eyes and tried not to look sour. I'd been hoping to avoid him today. The man seemed to be able to annoy me without even trying. Just the fact that he was here, wearing those low-slung board shorts and doing jet-ski tricks, drove me nuts. I hadn't even noticed him coming up the beach because I was busy playing with Spock.

"Hi, Tyler. Hello, Olivia," he greeted the two of us. "Is this the same dog from yesterday?"

"Yup. This is Spock. He's my dog," Tyler informed him. Spock ran over and licked Logan's hand. So much for the good sense of dogs.

Logan bent down and rubbed Spock's ears. He was

wearing a light gray t-shirt that clung to him like a second skin, as well as those ass-enhancing board shorts he had worn yesterday. They still looked flipping amazing on him. "He looks like a great dog."

"He's the best. I think I'm going to keep him." Tyler grinned. I was not looking forward to having this conversation with Maddy. I hoped Tyler had a plan to help Spock win his mom over.

"Good luck with that," Logan told him, as if he'd read my mind. "Have you taught him to play dead yet?"

Tyler shook his head. "I hadn't thought of that one."

Logan grinned. "His name's Spock, right? From Star Trek?" Tyler nodded enthusiastically. "Then, here's what we're going to teach him..."

Logan leaned forward and started whispering in Tyler's ear. I stood back and watched as a grin slowly overtook Tyler's face. Whatever Logan's idea was, Tyler loved it.

"Do you think you can teach him that?" Logan asked, stepping back.

"Definitely. Spock's smart." He rubbed the dog's head, and Spock's tail thumped against the sand. "I'm going to go work on it now. No watching, Aunt Liv- I'll show you when he's ready. You'll love it."

"If you need any help, you let me know," Logan offered. Still smiling ear to ear, Tyler picked up Spock's stick and started running. Together they sprinted down the beach to where they could practice his new trick without being seen. Logan and I stood quietly, watching the two of them run.

"What is this trick he's teaching his dog?" I asked as they went behind the storage shed.

"Not telling. It's pretty funny, though," Logan told me. He watched the shed for a moment as though he could see Tyler and Spock through it. "That dog is good for him."

"Yes, he is." I stared out at the storage shed, thinking

of how Tyler considered himself and the dog as the same. It broke my heart.

"Listen, I wanted to apologize for last night," Logan said after a moment of silence. "I didn't mean to bring up work on your vacation, and I'm sorry."

I narrowed my eyes. This had to be one of his tricks. "Sure."

"Seriously. I didn't mean anything by it." He grinned and held his hands up in front of him as if to show he wasn't armed. "I am here to relax, not to get you to sign anything. It's just a happy coincidence that we're both here."

"Right." I didn't fully believe that it was a happy coincidence, but I was at least willing to accept his apology.

"Let me make it up to you?" Logan asked. "Dinner. Tonight. Just you and me. No business, just give me the chance to really make up for what happened."

I chewed my inner cheek for a moment. I heard Spock bark and I turned to see him and Tyler sprinting down the beach toward us. He looked incredibly happy and proud.

It softened my heart to see Logan being so kind to Tyler. Plus, I couldn't forget that the man had saved my life, so maybe I owed him dinner without getting so defensive.

"Please?" Logan begged. I took a good look at him. The wind ruffled his messy hair as he smiled hopefully at me, making my heart speed up. He looked honest and open, yet sexy as hell. I just hoped it wasn't another trick.

"Fine," I conceded. "Because of what you've done for Tyler."

Logan beamed, making his brown eyes sparkle. It was impossible not to smile back. "You won't be sorry, I promise!"

"Do I need to wear anything special?" I asked. How

did I let myself get roped into this? I just hoped I wasn't going to get burned by him yet again. But, I knew deep down that I would fall for his tricks every time, no matter how burned I got. He just had that effect on me. I should have just steered clear of him from the beginning.

"No, just be comfortable. How does seven sound? I'll pick you up at your room," he answered. "I'm going to help you test out one of the resort's luxury opportunities."

"I hope you know that I'm not going to do the complimentary wedding ceremony," I teased. Logan laughed just as Tyler rejoined us.

"Why? Did he ask you?" Tyler quipped, looking back and forth between the two of us with confusion. Spock sat panting at his feet.

"No, just taking Olivia to dinner," Logan explained.

"Okay, good then. I didn't bring a suit." Tyler shot me a cheesy grin that made me roll my eyes. "And now, are you two ready for Spock's amazing new trick?"

"Incredibly. On the edge of my seat," I answered. Logan nodded enthusiastically.

"All right." Tyler grinned and turned to the dog. "Spock, do the needs of the many outweigh the needs of the few?"

Spock stared at Tyler for a moment, cocking his head as if he were trying really, really hard to understand English. Tyler nodded encouragingly at him, but Spock just wagged his tail.

"Spock, you had this a minute ago!" Tyler took a breath and then repeated the phrase. Spock just wagged his tail harder.

"Fine, we'll do it your way," Tyler conceded. He held the stick like a weapon and pointed it at Spock. "Pew, pew! You're dead!"

Spock promptly fell to his side and rolled up onto his back, sticking his legs up in the air and holding perfectly still. I giggled as Tyler completed the act with a long, "NOOOO" and ran to the dog's side. It would have been perfect, except Spock's tail started to wag as soon as Tyler touched him. Actually, that made it even better.

Logan and I applauded as Tyler and Spock took sitting positions before us in the sand.

"Even better than what I had in mind," Logan congratulated him. "I'm really impressed you taught him so fast."

"He's *really* smart," Tyler said with a grin as he hugged the dog to him. "Do you have any other ideas for tricks?"

"Teach him how to fetch your mom's slippers," I advised. "Possibly how to make coffee. It will make her like him more."

"I've got a couple more ideas if you want. How about tomorrow, we get together and I'll show you some of them?" Logan offered. Tyler eagerly nodded.

I thought about discouraging this friendship. Tyler was only going to get hurt when the billionaire decided that playing with kids wasn't his speed, but the fact that Tyler was excited and talking to another human being, besides his mother and me, was too good to make him stop.

I hoped that Logan understood the importance of what he was doing. Tyler hadn't spoken this much to anyone recently, and it was Logan's influence that was encouraging him. He never would have interacted with Izzy last night if Logan hadn't given him the vote of confidence earlier in the day. Logan had made him a hero and was now making him worthy of plans. I just hoped that he wouldn't let Tyler down as much as Tyler's father had.

"Okay, so I'll see Tyler tomorrow at ten," Logan said to Tyler and then grinned at me. "And I'll see you tonight at seven."

"Sounds good!" Tyler agreed. Spock wagged his tail. I nodded.

"Excellent." Logan flashed us one last smile before turning to head back toward the resort. He walked with a pep in his step I hadn't seen before as the wind plastered his shirt against his back. I shook my head as I tried to figure him out. He seemed legitimately excited about dinner tonight. I wondered just what he had planned. The resort had boasted several romantic excursion opportunities.

A gust of wind drove handfuls of sand into my bare legs. The waves out on the ocean had gotten rougher, and whitecaps crested with each swell. The storm was officially moving in, and the previously calm waters were now growing agitated.

"Come on, Tyler, we should head inside," I said, offering him my hand to get up. He took it, and I pulled him to standing. Another gale of wind came off of the ocean, lowering the temperature and making sand flurries in the air. "Let's go get cleaned up and have some lunch."

Tyler wiped some sand from the front of his shirt and did his best to brush most of the sticky, white grit from Spock. Even then, they were still incredibly dirty. "You think we'll be able to find a place to put Spock for the night? I don't want him out here in this."

"I'm sure if we ask the hotel, they'll have an idea. If nothing else, we'll sneak him into the garage or something," I assured him. Tyler nodded, and together the three of us headed back to the resort and out of the wind.

78

CHAPTER ELEVEN

"I have to run to the bathroom real quick," I told Tyler as we approached the resort's main building. "If you want, you can talk to the concierge and see if she knows a place where Spock can stay the night."

Tyler's brows pinched together slightly. He hated talking to strangers. "Okay."

I hurried across the lobby, fairly sure that he wasn't going to talk to the concierge. Tyler was incredibly shy. He had trouble answering the door for pizza, let alone talking to the hotel concierge. My sigh echoed off the marble surfaces in the bathroom. I quickly finished and washed my hands, prepping the mental speech to convince the concierge to help us find a place for Spock.

When I came out of the bathroom, I didn't see Tyler or Spock in the lobby. Glancing outside, I didn't see them there either, but the wind was picking up. I wondered if the storm was swinging further South than expected.

"Are you looking for Tyler and his dog?" the concierge asked, coming up behind me. I turned quickly to see a petite woman of Asian heritage smiling at me. She wore the resort's dark blue uniform and I recognized her as the usual person behind the concierge desk.

"Yes, I am, actually," I replied. "Where are they?"

"Tyler is getting the dog comfortable in one of the storage areas. We aren't using it right now and it's out of the storm," she explained. "I can show you to them, if you'll follow me."

She motioned behind the main desk toward a door I hadn't noticed before. She opened it and I stepped into a well-lit cement hallway.

"Where does this go?" I asked, glancing around as she continued on.. There were other corridors connecting to the main one, each junction marked with a map. It smelled like rain and wet cement the further in we went.

"All over the resort. This one connects the main building with the laundry facilities and storage. There are other tunnels that connect the kitchens, restaurants, and other maintenance buildings. They were all built specifically to adjoin everything in case of a hurricane, but we use them to move things around without having to bother guests." She turned at a yellow marker. "Here we are."

She opened a door revealing a concrete storage area. Tyler was busy making a bed out of towels while

Spock sniffed anxiously at the corners of the room.

"Thank you," I said to the concierge, stepping inside.

"Hi, Keiko," Tyler greeted the concierge. "Thank you again for the towels. I'll go see the chef for some food for Spock next."

"You are most welcome," Keiko said with a smile. "Is there anything else I can help you with?"

I shook my head, staring at Tyler. Aliens must have switched out the scared, shy kid with one who was able to talk to adults. I had never seen this side of him.

"No, thank you," Tyler replied. Keiko nodded and carefully closed the door behind her as she left.

"This looks like it will be a good place for Spock to stay," I said, petting lounging dog on his head. Tyler put the finishing touches on what was going to be Spock's bed before standing up.

"I think it will work. I'd like to have him in the hotel room with me, but I don't think Mom's ready for that yet." He glanced around the room. "I'm not sure Spock likes it, but it's way better than outside."

"How about we bring Spock back some food after lunch and see how he's doing in here," I offered. Tyler nodded.

"Do you mind if I talk to the chef first and meet you there? Keiko said the kitchen might have some plastic bowls I can use for water and food." Spock put his head under Tyler's hand, and Tyler rubbed his ears automatically. I could hear the wind outside even through the thick concrete.

I blinked twice in surprise. This was the second

time he was going to stand up for the dog and get over his shyness around strangers. "Um, sure. That's fine by me. Do you want me to come with you to talk to the chef?"

"No, that's okay. I got it," he told me. He smiled and went to the door. "You be good, Spock. I'll be back in a little bit with lunch."

Spock tried to follow, and we had to slam the door shut in order to keep him in the room alone. Spock cried softly at the door, begging us to come back and rescue him.

"You think he'll be okay?" Tyler asked, glancing back at the door as we walked down the hallway. "He sounded scared."

I smiled and hugged him around the shoulders. "He'll be fine. We'll make lunch fast."

He nodded, and we hurried down the hallway. Maddy wasn't going to like the idea of a dog, but if Spock was getting Tyler over his shyness and insecurities, she was going to warm up to the idea of a pet quickly. If this was what Spock was able to do for Tyler's confidence after just a day, I couldn't wait to see what he would do for him after a week, a month, even a year. Maddy was just going to have to deal with it.

***

I came out of the shower with my hair wrapped in a towel and my body nestled in a fluffy hotel robe. It felt good to be clean. I had helped Tyler carry water and food to Spock and tried to help Tyler brush the sand out of Spock's fur after lunch. I was fairly certain that the dog was still half sand. Now that it was approaching dinner time, Tyler was probably back in the storage room with Spock. Maddy had been less than thrilled about it all, but she was excited to see the changes it was bringing about in Tyler.

I glanced at my watch. It was only a couple minutes after six, so I still had plenty of time to get ready for my date with Logan. I grabbed my makeup bag and stood in front of the mirror.

No, I told myself. *Not a date.* I did not want to get romantically involved with him again. He had a body that made my insides heat and quiver, but the fact that he had burned me so badly before still stung. I wasn't about to let him get close enough to hurt me again.

Then why are you going to dinner? I frowned and noticed little lines popping up on my face. Logan Hayes had betrayed me once before. He had almost ruined everything I had been trying to build and didn't even have the decency to call me himself to do it.

Even so, he was good for Tyler. The past couple of days, Logan had gotten more conversation and smiles out of him than I had seen in weeks. For whatever reason, Tyler trusted him. And so far, he hadn't betrayed that trust.

I set the brush down hard on the bathroom counter. I really had no idea what I was doing when it came to Logan.

"I'll just cancel," I said out-loud to the mirror. "I shouldn't have dinner with the competition anyway."

Yet, I kept putting on my makeup and didn't pick up the phone to call and cancel. Part of me, probably the part of me that enjoyed seeing him walk in his board shorts, wanted to go to dinner with him. If I ignored the past, the man was a catch. Billionaire, gorgeous, and apparently good with kids and dogs. It was just the way he had used me two years ago that burned.

The TV buzzed with an important update in the other room. I had forgotten to turn it off when I got in the shower.

"The National Hurricane Center has officially upgraded Tropical Storm Hannah to a Category 1 hurricane." A pretty forecaster stood in front of a map with a large swirl of clouds spinning across the ocean. "The storm is expected to skirt the edge of Antigua and surrounding islands, but as always, residents are encouraged to take precautions. These storms can shift direction or increase in power at any time."

The wind rattled the boards over my window as if to accentuate her words. The resort staff had been busy all day preparing everything for the oncoming storm. All the windows had boards, and even the sliding glass doors had been protected. It looked as though the staff were getting ready for a Category 5 rather than a storm that was supposed to bypass us, but I would rather they be over-prepared than surprised.

I looked back to the mirror to find I had finished my makeup without realizing it. What was I doing? I should know better than to even go to dinner with him. I had been down this road before. I slid my earrings on, thinking about the past and the last time I had gone out with Logan Hayes.

CHAPTER TWELVE

Two years ago

After our meeting earlier today, I couldn't stop thinking about Logan. The warm caramel swirls of his eyes. That one golden curl that I wanted to sweep off his forehead. That smile that made me purr like a cat in sunshine. Just thinking about him had me flustered in the best way. There was a connection between the two of us that wasn't just strictly business. At least, I really, really hoped there was.

Especially because I had already picked out a backless black dress to wear out tonight.

My phone buzzed, and I held my breath as I looked at the caller ID. It was a number I didn't recognize. *Please, please, please...*

"Hello?" I sounded far more breathless than I had

intended.

"Olivia?" It was Logan. A little shiver of anticipation went down my spine. I liked the way my name sounded in his rich, masculine voice.

"This is she," I replied, trying to sound like I didn't recognize the voice. I didn't want to appear too eager.

"Hi, it's Logan. From earlier today," he said with a small laugh. He sounded almost nervous, which made the butterflies in my stomach far more hopeful than they had any right to be. "Would you still be interested in getting a drink with me tonight?"

"I'd love to," I said, grinning into the phone. I was imagining his reciprocal smile on the other side of the line. "Where would you like to meet?"

"Have you ever been to de Luxe? I have a standing reservation there we can use," he asked. My jaw dropped a little. It was only the most exclusive, expensive and infamous club in Chicago.

"No," I answered. "But I know where it is."

"Would you be able to meet me there in half an hour? Just tell the bouncer you're meeting me and you won't have to wait in line," he said, as if walking into de Luxe was something normal.

"I can do that." I was bouncing up and down on the couch and trying very hard to keep my voice steady. "I'll see you there."

"Great!" He sounded excited as well. "See you soon!"

I hung up the phone, stared at it for a moment and then let out a whoop that made the neighbor's dog start barking. I was going to go to de Luxe with Logan Hayes!

Twenty-five minutes later, I was stepping out of a cab in front of the most exclusive club in the city. The line to get in wound around the block, but I walked past them all to get to the front door. A big man with sunglasses, even though it was almost dark out, stood guard over the entrance. I swallowed hard and went up to him, hoping I was giving off an aura of importance. The people in line stared at me, and I could hear whispers as I approached.

"Excuse me," I said, putting as much confidence in my voice as I could muster. "I'm Olivia Statler. I'm here to meet Mr. Logan Hayes."

When the man didn't move a muscle, I nearly took a step back. Maybe he wasn't here yet, or I had gotten the address wrong.

The big guard slowly looked down at the guest list, and his face immediately softened as he read it. "Right this way, Ms. Statler." He moved to the side and lowered the red velvet rope to let me in. I heard at least two gasps from the line as I bypassed everyone in it. The man had a warm smile that changed him from incredibly intimidating to teddy bear for the two seconds he let me see it.

I stepped into the entryway and could see the main room. It was romantically lit, with silver couches and glowing tables. Music thrummed through the building, and the dance floor was already alive with dancers.

"Ms. Statler?" A woman in a flattering silver dress suit tapped my shoulder and motioned me to follow her. She took me up a flight of stairs, past an even bigger security guard, and into the VIP lounge. Logan was waiting for me at a table overlooking the dance floor. He stood as soon as he saw me, a grin nearly splitting his face in two.

"You look spectacular," he said appreciatively, his eyes traversing my figure at least twice. I blushed, but I didn't mind that he was looking. In fact, I rather liked the idea that he was.

"Thanks." I sat down at the table and looked him over. "You look pretty spectacular yourself."

He beamed and shrugged as if it were nothing. He had changed into a black suit and smoothed his hair back. The overall effect was one of rugged sophistication, and it looked damn good on him.

"I took the liberty of ordering a bottle of champagne. Do you like Dom Perignon?" He pulled out a bottle from an ice bucket sitting on the table that I hadn't noticed.

"I've never had it," I said, shaking my head.

"Then, now is a perfect time to try something new." He handed me a glass and poured out the golden liquid. I took a careful sip, and the bubbles tickled my nose. "What do you think?"

"Honestly?" I set my glass down on the table and looked at it. "I hate to say this, but it just tastes like plain old champagne to me. I don't taste anything special about it. I guess I'm a terrible champagne drinker."

Logan laughed, making me feel completely at ease. "It took me a long time to taste the difference, but half the fun is just ordering it and watching peoples' reactions."

I took another sip to steady my nerves. I was

having a hard time not staring at him. "Have you spoken with your father yet?"

"No," he said, shaking his head. "I have a meeting with him tomorrow. I'm very hopeful about it, though. Your idea is perfect for Travel, Inc. I'm really looking forward to getting to work with you."

"Me too," I replied, feeling a blush warming my cheeks. I wanted to do more than just work with him. I looked up at him, and the look on his face said he wanted more too. The fact that we were out for drinks before he spoke to his father implied that this wasn't a business meeting. The butterflies in my stomach danced for joy, and I took another sip of champagne to quiet them.

"So," he said, clearing his throat. "You said you've never been here before? Not on a date or anything?"

"I've been so busy getting my business started that I haven't had time to go on dates," I explained. I paused to take another sip of champagne and looked up coyly from my drink. "If you're trying to find out, I'm not currently seeing anyone."

Logan coughed a little on his drink, blushing slightly. He patted his chest and cleared his throat. "That's good to know," he said with a smirk. "I'm glad to know I didn't get dressed up for nothing."

Now it was my turn to blush. There was a silence for a moment as our eyes remained locked. "So?" I asked.

"So, what?" he asked back.

"So... are you currently seeing anyone?"

He laughed and my heart fluttered. "Ms. Statler, you haven't done your research very well."

My jaw dropped a little bit. "I could say the same about you! Besides, I only looked up your company, not you. I thought that was the most polite way about doing things."

He shrugged. "Maybe. Maybe I already knew that you weren't seeing anyone."

I laughed as I rolled my eyes, then I looked back at him. His look was a little too serious. I lifted my eyebrows, as if to ask the question again.

"Yes, Olivia, I'm single," he said with a smile. He looked at the curtain over the balcony at the dance floor. "And now that that business is out of the way, here's a question I couldn't find the answer to. Do you dance?"

I glanced down at the dance floor. People were dancing and gyrating below us. Everyone was having a great time. "Oh, no. No way."

He laughed. "What's the matter? Didn't have fun in college?"

I laughed and threw back the rest of my glass of champagne. When I put the glass down, I said, "I had plenty of fun in college. This just wasn't my scene."

"What about now?" he asked.

"Now?"

"Do you have fun now?"

I laughed again. "Sometimes it seems like all I do is work. But, yes, I have fun."

"Okay, then let's have some fun." He stood, holding his hand out for me. I smiled and accepted it, letting him lead the way as I slowly walked behind him in my heels. He moved with a smooth confidence that I enjoyed watching. Even after he got us past the curtain to the VIP room, the crowd seemed to part for him as he walked toward the stairs.

Both of us were getting glances from the entire floor, and I knew exactly why. We were a sexy couple, even if we weren't technically together. I wasn't used to the attention, but I enjoyed their looks.

We slowly descended the stairs and Logan continued to lead me toward the dance floor. I was actually getting pretty nervous by the time we finally made our way past the last table and onto the raised floor. He didn't stop there, though, he kept going, straight toward the center of the dance floor, melting into the crowd.

When he got to his destination, he turned to me. His eyes gave me a quick once-over, a hungry glance, before he leaned in and put his hands on my hips. Immediately, I could feel them gripping me through the soft fabric of my dress.

My hips began to sway as he guided me through the motions, keeping in perfect time with the tempo. I never considered myself to be a good dancer, but it was easy with Logan. My body responded to his, finding the rhythm of the music as it thrummed through me. I could help but look down at his hips moving, wondering what they'd look like without those fantastic pants on top of them, thrusting to the beat of the music. The thought shocked me a little bit, so I looked back into his eyes. They were still looking at me with that hungry look.

I didn't look away. I looked right back at him, putting my hand over his shoulder and drawing him in closer to me. We seemed to be matched in perfect time for a moment. Even when the song changed, he didn't seem to miss a beat, just changing his tempo as we continued to dance.

It was a perfect moment. Too perfect, it seemed. An exotic looking woman in a tight dress danced over near us. She ignored me as she put her hands in her hair and began to dance up against Logan, showing him just how interested she was. My mouth dropped as I looked at her, and she gave me a quick look like she had already decided that she didn't care what I thought. She was absolutely supermodel gorgeous and she was going after Logan like a lioness. She didn't even consider me a threat.

Logan surprised me. Normally I would expect a man to react, positively or negatively. I expected him to turn and either begin to dance with her or tell her that he wasn't interested. However, his eyes never left my body. His hands never left my sides. He completely ignored her, acting like she didn't exist. Even when she leaned in and whispered something in his ear, he never reacted. He was fixated on me.

The woman stared at him confused, frozen as the music beat around her. She certainly wasn't expecting that reaction. She finally shook herself before huffing off like a wet cat. Logan's gaze still pierced into me, completely oblivious to the other woman. I had never felt this sexy in my life. Logan Hayes had turned down a gorgeous woman for me.

Hope and excitement bubbled up inside of me. He liked me, hopefully as much as I liked him. It wasn't just a physical connection either. It could have just been my imagination, but I felt like there was a bond between us. Something that would last past the songs of the evening and into the future. From the way he looked at me, he felt it too.

Maybe it was the alcohol, but I wanted him so badly at that moment. The music and the way my body was responding to his had me wanting to push this further. I knew we had an intellectual connection, but right now, the physical one was overpowering. I leaned in, grinding into him a little bit more. I put my hands in my hair as the other woman had done, turning around slowly. His hands moved up and down my sides, exploring me in ways that excited me.

While his left hand remained on my hip, his right hand moved up my back. I shivered as his fingers met the bare skin of my neck, moving up into my hair. He grabbed a handful and gripped me. It wasn't pulling, it was guiding me, and it was so incredibly sexy.

A voice whispered in my ear. "I've never met any girl who could make me react like you."

I couldn't help but moan, both in lust and in acknowledgment.

"No woman I've ever met has ever had the sense of humor, the business acumen, and the raw sexual energy that you have."

I giggled. "You sure know how to talk to a girl."

His voice turned very low. "So it's working?"

I decided to answer by pressing back into him. When I felt how hard he had gotten through his pants, I knew that he wanted exactly what I did. He inhaled sharply as I began to grind up against him.

I turned around to face him again. His hand was still in my hair, and I fell into him. He smelled so good, like clean soap and a light, woodsy cologne. My eyes flutter shut as I lifted onto my tiptoes and kissed him. It started light, but quickly became more as kissed me back. We continued to dance on the floor, kissing and swaying to the beat of the music, for a few long minutes. It was heaven.

He broke from the kiss. "Have you ever been in a limo?" he whispered into my ear, his hands tightening on my waist. I loved how I felt with him touching me.

"No," I replied slowly, my eyes still closed from the kiss.

"Want to take a ride in mine?" he asked.

My eyes shot open. *What kind of girl did he take me for?* I thought. However, when I saw the look on his face, the sheer lust and desire that he felt, I knew I couldn't say no. I was exactly that kind of girl when it came to him.

I nodded my head quickly. In a moment, his hand was on mind, leading me back through the club.

CHAPTER THIRTEEN

෧෯෧

Two years earlier

We stepped out the back door and walked past the limo driver, who was flirting with one of the club's waitresses. He started to follow after us, but Logan waved him off. The driver shrugged and returned to smiling at the pretty girl as we hurried across the dark parking lot to the limo.

Logan opened the door, tucking his free arm behind him and standing at attention as if he were escorting royalty. I giggled and slid across the leather seats into the vehicle. I had never been in a limo before, and it took me a moment to soak it all in. The seats were made of white leather and wrapped three-quarters of the limo in comfort. The fourth side was a bar, complete with champagne, glasses, and an assortment of mixers and booze. The ceiling was composed of blue lights and mirrors that cast the entire back seat in sexy shadows.

Giddy butterflies danced around in my stomach. It had been a while since I had been with a man, and an even longer while since I had been this attracted to one. I hoped that we were going to do what I thought we were going to do. I had never had a one-night-stand-- not even in college-- but there was just something about Logan that made me want him and trust him. Being with him felt like instinct and didn't require any thought. It felt right.

Logan sat down beside me and closed the door behind him. He reached over and hit a couple of buttons on a panel, which turned on some low, sultry jazz and raised the privacy window. Our knees bumped as we sat on the shorter seat at the very rear of the limo. Now that we were here-- now we were actually about to do this-- I was suddenly nervous. What if he didn't like me as much as I liked him?

I turned to kiss him just as he reached for me. Instead of meeting in a sensuous, passionate kiss, we bumped noses and missed the kiss entirely. I could feel a blush radiate from my forehead down to my toes.

Thankfully, Logan laughed. "So much for me being suave," he joked, instantly taking away any embarrassment. He shrugged out of his jacket and folded it over the back of the seat. "Shall we try again?"

I nodded, grinning like a love-struck idiot. He put his thumb to my cheek and lightly curled his fingers against my jaw. Gently, he drew me to him, guiding our mouths together in a sweet and sensual kiss. It was deep and hungry as he tasted me completely before pulling back to look at me. He had such beautiful eyes. They were warm and dark like velvet, and with burning golden embers scattered throughout that enveloped me completely. A girl would do just about anything to be lost in those eyes.

His hand went to my back as I leaned forward to taste him again, pressing my leg against his. I loved the way his palm and fingers caressed my skin, stopping only when they hit the silky black fabric at my lower back. I started to unbutton his shirt, working my way up from the bottom with careful fingers. The creamy fabric opened easily, revealing his smooth, muscular chest underneath.

Placing my palms on his pectoral muscles, I could feel his heart pounding in his chest. It was beating just as hard as mine was. The idea that this confident, charming man could be as excited and nervous as I was gave me a strange sort of courage. Maybe he did like me after all.

I pushed the shirt from his shoulders, and he helped me remove it completely. I stared at his broad shoulders and chest, my mouth going dry with lust. He was gorgeous. Absolutely gorgeous. They say that sometimes the suit makes the man, but in this case, the man made the suit. Logan looked even more amazing without his shirt than I ever could have imagined. For a moment, I felt self-conscious about the padding around my middle, but then I looked up into his eyes and realized that he didn't see it. He was looking at me like I was some sort of creamy, delicious dessert.

A tattoo just above his heart caught my eye. In a flowing font that could only be a woman's handwriting, the words "All my love" were marked on his chest. I traced them with my finger, feeling the pulse of his heart underneath.

"It's for my mom," he said, answering my unspoken question. "She wrote that on the bottom of the last birthday card she gave me. When she died, I wanted a part of her to always be with me."

There was an ache deep in my chest for his loss. I had read enough about Travel, Inc. to know that Logan's mother had helped his father start the company and then died in a tragic car accident when Logan was just a boy. The fact that none of the Hayes men ever talked about her in public spoke to the pain they still felt from her passing. Touching her words, I knew I was now part of a very elite few.

"It's a beautiful tribute," I said quietly.

I looked up at Logan's face. There was just a hint of sadness, but he didn't move my hand from his mother's words. "I think she would have liked you," he replied. Smiling, he banished any remaining traces of sadness from his eyes. "Do you have any tattoos?"

I shook my head. "No, I almost got a butterfly on my lower back when I turned eighteen, but I didn't have a good reason for it, other than being eighteen. But then I realized that I wouldn't care about being eighteen in a year, but that tattoo would be with me forever. I decided then that my tattoos should have meaning. Like yours."

I touched the words on his chest again. Logan

reached down and took my chin in his fingers, raising my face to look at him. He smiled, soft and sweet. It melted what was left of my heart into a puddle. Slowly, he pulled me to him and kissed me again.

I closed my eyes and reveled in his kiss. I didn't want to open them; I was afraid that this was a dream and I would wake up at any moment to find that this sexy, handsome, funny man was all in my imagination. I didn't even care that he was insanely wealthy. He liked me and found me attractive. Stubborn, perfectionist, goofy me. It had to be a dream.

The intensity of the kiss increased in intensity from tender to insistent. Heat and passion erupted from our lips. Logan's hands went again to the skin on my back like he couldn't get enough of it. His every movement made me hotter. I wanted him so badly I could barely think. His mouth was firm and hungry, his tongue caressing mine like he couldn't get enough of my taste.

I pulled back, gasping for breath. Logan's eyes burned with desire, drawing me to him like a moth to the flame. I reached behind me and tugged on the short zipper that held my dress together. Logan's pupils dilated as the tight fabric loosened. I held it to my chest for a moment, my heart speeding out of control. This was the moment of truth. I let the dress fall. He stared, open mouthed and completely enthralled.

"You are so damn beautiful," he finally whispered, raising his eyes from my body. I blushed. The look on his face made me feel incredibly feminine and wanted.

Desire poured from him as I tugged on the hem and wiggled out of the dress, leaving nothing behind but my heels and a pretty little lacy panty.

As Logan let out a strained breath, a thrill went through me. Granted, I wasn't the most experienced girl in the world, but no man had ever looked at me like that. His reaction was genuine and empowering. I could easily see the effect I was having on him, and it made me want him all the more.

I kissed him, this time pressing my bare chest against his. He groaned into my lips, wrapping his strong arms around me and pulling me more tightly against him. I shifted my legs, lifting one and sliding it across his lap until I was straddling him. The bulge of his erection pressed through his pants and up toward the lace of my underwear. I rocked gently against him, wanting to do far more than just that.

Cupping one of my breasts in his palm, he stroked my nipple with his thumb until it grew taut. A string of desire ran straight from that nipple into the depths of my core and sent vibrations of lust throughout my whole being. I couldn't stop my hands from tracing down the line of his stomach, lower and lower to his waistline. It only took me a moment to undo the belt and the button below it so I could slide my hand into his pants.

We both gasped as I touched him. He was hard and ready. I caressed the stretched fabric of his briefs, feeling the heat and strength of his erection increase with every touch. His visceral reaction turned me on more than I could imagine. It made me braver, made me want more, made me take more.

"Lie down," he commanded, putting his hands on my hips. I cocked my head, and he grinned, lifting me off of him and onto the longer limo seat. He pushed his pants down, kicking them and his shoes to the side as he knelt on the floor by my feet. Excitement bubbled in my stomach at the wonderful things he could do from that position.

With strong hands, he bent one of my legs up on the seat and spread the other wide so my foot touched the floor. I was deliciously exposed to him. With a feather-light touch, he ran his fingers up from sensitive skin of my inner thigh, up to the lacy edge of my panties. Just feeling his fingers brush across my most erogenous zone made me gasp. He chuckled, and did it again.

I lay my head back and watched his reflection in the blue mirrors of the ceiling as he pulled on the stretchy lace band and slowly removed my underwear. I lay bare for him, wearing nothing but heels and a smile as he spread my legs further and dipped his head to taste me.

The first lick was wet and warm and sent me shooting into the stratosphere with pleasure. He hummed and teased, using his tongue, lips and teeth to deliver the most exquisite torture. I arched and writhed under his touch, but he never stopped pushing me to the edge of what I could tolerate. The fire he had started within me was flashing with white heat, and the deep need to be filled growing more insistent. I skittered over the edge of oblivion, gasping as I froze and shook, lost to the erotic waves coursing through every fiber of my being.

When I came back to my senses, the ache to be filled, to have him inside of me was unbearable. I would have done anything to have him complete me.

"Please," I whimpered, raising my head to look at his handsome face. "I want you."

The air was charged with electric anticipation. My eyes drifted across his face, letting the hunger for him show through. He nodded sharply, reaching for his pants. In less than a heartbeat, he had his briefs off and a condom ready. I couldn't take my eyes from his body, watching as he came closer and then slowly prepared to join me.

It was heaven. He filled me to the hilt, sliding in and out to a slow, sensual beat that drove me wild. I arched and writhed against his strength, gasping his name as he filled me again and again. He was like no other lover I had ever had. He completed me in the most physical and carnal way possible.

He panted, increasing his rhythm as lust overtook him. With a sweet shock, I realized it was me that was making him pant, making him lose himself. I shuddered against him, letting him claim me for his own. Sweet climax washed over me, and I cried out in ecstasy. He took my body and gave me his in return. Logan's low, ragged groan answered my cry as he followed me over the edge and into pure pleasure.

Slowly, I opened my eyes and found him smiling warmly down at me. I had to consciously relax my hands from his back; I had been clinging to him with a desperation that surprised me. I never wanted this moment to end. Here in his arms, I was safe and warm. I felt loved, though I knew it was too early for me to have the right to say it out loud.

"Logan?" I murmured, enjoying the way his name felt on my lips.

"Hmm?" he answered, smiling down at me with those beautiful brown eyes.

"That was wonderful," which was a complete understatement. There was no word in the human language that described just how wonderful it had been.

"I agree." He shifted his weight slightly, giving me more space but still staying within me. I never wanted him to leave me. The corners of his mouth quirked up in a cocky grin. "Can I call you again? I know this great little Italian restaurant with an even better parking lot."

I giggled. "That would be great."

He kissed me gently before slowly moving away. I ached for more as he left me, wanting to be close to him forever. He rummaged through the bar until he found some napkins. Together we cleaned up and slowly put our clothes back on. I wondered if the limo driver was in the front seat yet or if he was still flirting with the waitress.

"Do you want to go back in?" Logan asked, helping me zip my dress.

I opened my mouth to answer, but instead a jaw-cracking yawn escaped. I pressed my hand to my mouth. "Sorry."

He smiled. "No, you're fine."

"I was nervous about our meeting, so I didn't sleep very well last night. I guess it's catching up with me. It's just been a busy day," I admitted.

"It's been a great day," he corrected.

I grinned at him. "Better than great." And then I yawned again. "I'm so sorry!"

"Don't be," he reassured me. "Let me take you home."

"Okay," I said, settling into one of the seats of the limo, suddenly very sleepy. "Who knows, maybe I'll even invite you up."

Logan went to the door and opened it, sticking his head out and waving to the limo driver. It took a moment, but I soon heard the door open and shut as the driver returned. Logan lowered the privacy screen.

"Where to, sir?" the driver asked as soon as it was down.

The limo's engine purred to life as I recited my address. The lights dimmed, and Logan wrapped his arm around me as we started moving. Everything was comfortable and warm. I felt protected and wanted. Maybe even loved. I had never felt this strongly about someone before, nor had I ever imagined I could feel so deeply so soon. I actually felt happy instead of guilty about our horizontal tango, which was a first for me. I really, *really* liked him. It surprised me, but it felt right. Logan felt right. We belonged together.

I rested my head against Logan's shoulder, unable to stay upright. The day's events had finally caught up to me. Throw in some mind-blowing sex, and I was amazed I still had the energy to breathe. Even though I didn't mean to, I couldn't help dozing off, lulled by the engine and Logan's warmth.

"Where are your keys?" Logan asked gently, waking me as we arrived at my apartment.

"Purse," I murmured, my tongue thick with sleep. "The gold key's for the front door and the silver one undoes the deadbolt on my apartment... 2B..."

I heard the jingle of my keys and then I was in Logan's arms. He lifted me as though I were a child, carrying me out of the limo and up the stairs to my apartment. I could hear the driver mumbling my instructions of gold and silver keys as he opened the doors ahead of us. I was glad Logan was carrying me. I was so tired, I fell asleep again in his arms on the way up the stairs.

The next thing I knew was the soft, welcoming embrace of my mattress. Logan carefully took off my shoes and neatly placed them on the floor by my bed before pulling the covers up to my chin. Deep sleep was beckoning me forward, but I struggled to stay awake to say goodnight. A beam of light from the living room shone on his handsome face.

"Shh," Logan whispered, soothing me back to sleep. He smoothed my hair from my face and gently kissed my forehead. "Sweet dreams, Olivia."

He closed the door behind him, taking the light with him, and I quickly lost myself again to dreams.

≈≈≈ ≈≈≈

CHAPTER FOURTEEN

Present Day

"Coming up at seven, news from the Middle East..."

I clicked the TV off. I had exactly fifteen minutes before Logan was supposed to arrive. Butterflies danced in my stomach, and I couldn't keep the smile off my face as I slid on my favorite cotton sundress. It was a deep red that darkened to purple as it descended to just above my knees. I had no reason to look forward to dinner with Logan, but I couldn't help it. My body and brain remembered two very different Logans, and right now, my body was remembering harder. I could almost feel his fingers on my skin again, the way his body had felt pressed against mine. I wanted to believe he hadn't meant to hurt me, that all the heartache had been an accident. I wanted to believe that it could turn out better this time.

My cellphone started to ring on my nightstand. Since this was a business trip, I had left it on. I was intending to leave it in my room for dinner, but as I still had a few minutes to wait, I picked it up.

"Olivia? It's me, Susan," the voice on the other line said. Susan was my best consultant and the manager of the other five home consultants. She was in charge of running things while Maddy and I were on vacation. My smile faded. She was only supposed to call if there were problems.

"Is something wrong?" I asked, hoping that she was just overreacting to something that didn't matter.

"I'm really sorry to bother you on your vacation, but..." Susan hesitated, and I could practically hear her biting her lip.

"What is it, Susan?" Panic was starting to rise in my throat, and the butterflies in my stomach were now dancing to a very different beat.

"Four of our consultants just quit," she blurted out. It took me a moment, but my knees figured out this was bad news before my brain did and I sank onto the bed.

"What?" I asked, not because I didn't hear her, but because I couldn't believe what I'd heard. "Why?"

"I asked, and they said they weren't supposed to say, but I leaned on Melissa, and she spilled." Susan took a deep breath. I knew I wasn't going to like what she was going to say. "They were offered positions at

Travel, Inc. Same job, but way more money."

"Are you serious?" This couldn't be happening. I couldn't wrap my head around it. I paid more than average because I wanted to retain the best travel consultants. I couldn't believe Travel, Inc. would stoop this low.

"Yeah. I wasn't sure if she was telling the truth, but then I got a phone call about thirty minutes ago offering the same thing to me. The pay is substantially more, and they wanted us to start right away. No two weeks' notice or anything," she told me. I could hear the stress in her voice. "I want you to know, I didn't take it. You have been the best boss I've ever had, and I didn't feel right about it."

"Thank you, Susan. I really appreciate that," I replied mechanically. I was reeling. This couldn't be happening.

"I know you're on vacation, but I figured you should know. I'm really sorry, but I figured this fell under the 'call you if there's an emergency' clause. I sent you an email with all their notices." Susan sounded dejected. She knew as well as I did that this would be a devastating blow to my business. Without consultants, I didn't have the concierge personalization part of my travel agency. It would take weeks to hire and train new ones.

"You did the right thing." I took a deep breath and pinched the bridge of my nose. "Who left?"

"Lisa, Joan, Amber, and Stacy. Diane said they called, but she turned them down."

"Shit," I whispered. Joan and Amber were my best up-sellers. "This is bad. I'll be on the next flight home."

"What about your vacation?" Susan asked, surprise in her voice.

"If I don't have consultants making these bookings, then I don't have a business. Without a business, no vacations." I stood up and grabbed my empty suitcase, throwing it on the bed. "This is low, even for Travel, Inc."

"I'm really sorry, Olivia," Susan said. I knew she meant it too.

"It's not your fault. I'll call you once I have a flight," I told her. Clicking off the phone, I stopped and stared at my suitcase, my vision blurring with tears.

I couldn't believe Logan had done this to me...again. I was about to spend an wonderful evening with him, and he'd already managed to ruin it. Again. I wondered if he was even planning on telling me what he had done or if he was just looking for a good time.

I angrily threw some clothes in the suitcase before getting distracted and instead turned to my computer to open up the email from Susan. All four resignations were there. I hit print and called Maddy.

"Maddy, Travel, Inc.'s trying to ruin us. I have to get home. Will you get me on the next flight back? I don't care how much it costs."

"Sure," Maddy answered. "I'm actually at my computer now. What's going on?"

"Four of our consultants just quit. They have jobs at Travel, Inc. now," I said softly. It felt horrible to say it out loud.

"What?" Maddy squawked. I heard the phone hit the desk and then the scramble for her to pick it up. "How is that possible?"

"I don't know, but I'm going to get to the bottom of it." Shock had now graduated to anger.

"The earliest I can get you is a flight out at nine tomorrow morning," she said. I could hear her clicking on her computer. "There are warnings that it might be delayed due to weather, but you're all booked."

"Thanks. I don't care as long as I can get home to fix this mess. I'll forward you what's happening," I said, picking up the freshly-printed letters.

"Do you need me to come too? Tyler and I can be packed and ready to go in no time," she offered.

"No," I told her. "I can handle it. No reason for all of us to suffer. Besides, this vacation has been so good for Tyler. You two stay."

"Okay," she said with a hint of relief in her voice. "Weren't you supposed to have dinner with Logan tonight? I thought Tyler said something along those lines..."

"We were. I'm going to go ask him about this now." My hands shook with fury. I couldn't believe he would do this me.

"Don't kill him," Maddy replied, only half-joking. "But if you do, I'll help you hide the body. This storm will make the perfect cover."

I smiled quickly and hung up the phone. With proof of what his company had done, I stalked out in the hall to confront Logan.

It felt like a strange repeat of the past, only this time, I'd let him know just how I felt.

CHAPTER FIFTEEN

2 Years Earlier...

I stretched out, surprised to find myself in my own bed. I vaguely remembered Logan asking me about my keys, but I didn't remember putting myself under the covers. I lifted the sheet and found I was still wearing my dress from the night before.

I stumbled out of bed and into the kitchen. For a moment, I hoped I would find Logan asleep on my couch, but the living room was empty. However, sitting on the kitchen counter was a piece of paper. Logan's messy handwriting filled the page.

Dear Olivia,

Thank you for the wonderful evening. I can't remember the last time I had so much fun with someone. It was one of the best nights of my life.

Here is my personal phone number. Feel free to call me anytime.

-Logan

I smiled down at the note. Warm, fuzzy feelings floated through me like marshmallows in hot chocolate. For once, things seemed to be working out the way they were supposed to. I could finally feel success coming my way.

I turned on the coffee machine and went to start the shower. I still smelled like him. I almost didn't want to lose that scent, but the rest of me did not smell so nice. Plus, my hair and makeup now looked like something out of a scary movie. I stepped under the warm water, feeling the night wash free.

I'll have him again, I thought to myself. It made me shiver with anticipation. I wanted to wrap myself up in his arms again. I replayed the night in my head, humming happily as I washed my hair. I loved the way his eyes had glowed with want, but there was something more there. I knew I was falling hard for him.

Be honest, I scolded myself. *You fell for him the moment you saw him.* I knew it was true. I wasn't the type of girl who believed in love at first sight, but then, I also wasn't the type of girl who had sex in the backseat of a limo on the first date, either. We had just connected so well. I could see us actually working out.

My phone rang in the other room, but my hair was full of shampoo suds. I realized I had been standing under the water for twenty minutes without doing anything but thinking of Logan. I ducked under the water and quickly finished up my shower. I hoped the call was from Logan, even though it hadn't been the requisite three days the movies all claimed he should wait.

With a towel wrapped around my head, I picked up my phone. I had one missed call, but it unfortunately wasn't from Logan. It was from WorldofTravelAgents.com, one of the bigger companies interested in buying my business. I hesitated for a moment before calling them back, apprehension and excitement running through me.

It wasn't official that Travel, Inc. was going to buy me out, but given what happened last night, I was pretty sure it was going to happen. One didn't sleep with the COO and not get certain perks. I was going to have to tell the other companies that Travel, Inc. was buying me out eventually. I decided to give into my excitement from last night and share the news.

"Hello, Mr. Carmichael," I greeted the man who answered. "Just calling you back."

"Olivia," Mr. Carmichael said warmly. "I was just calling to see if you had given our offer some more thought."

"Actually, I'm going to have to decline," I said, trying to keep the excitement out of my voice. "Travel, Inc. is ready to start negotiations. I should be signing paperwork this afternoon."

"Travel, Inc.? That's fantastic!" Mr. Carmichael sounded genuinely excited for me. "From the minute I met you and saw your business plan, I knew you were destined for great things. If Travel, Inc. wants you, there's no way I can compete with what they can offer. Congratulations!"

"Thank you, Mr. Carmichael." I was blushing and very glad he couldn't see me through the phone. "I really appreciate it. I want you to know that I was very interested in your proposal."

"Thank you, but Travel, Inc. really will give your business the boost it deserves. I'm so very happy for you," he congratulated me. "If I were in your shoes, I would be dancing up and down the street. Let me know if you're ever thinking of acquiring more partners. I'd love to have Travel, Inc. as a resource."

"I will keep you in mind," I told him. "Thank you, again."

"My pleasure, Olivia. Good luck with Travel, Inc.," he said and we both hung up.

I set the phone back on my nightstand and grinned. Things were definitely going my way.

I threw on some clothes and pulled out my laptop. I wanted to start implementing some of the ideas Logan had given me last night while I waited for his call. As I worked, I realized what a gift he had given me with his insights. Some of the issues he had found would have caused some serious delays. He had shortened the learning curve on several of my implementation ideas. I couldn't wait to pick his brain again and learn even more.

I opened up my internet browser to check my email while I waited for my other programs to finish loading. After a few minutes, I laughed as I realized I had opened up his website and had been staring at his company picture. Even on the computer screen, his eyes were mesmerizing and bathed me in their warmth. I hoped we could celebrate Dream Vacations joining Travel, Inc. tonight. I was even thinking of running out to my favorite lingerie shop to make sure I had something special to wear for the occasion.

"Get back to work," I chided myself softly, closing the webpage. There was still so much for me to do. He'd call when he was ready. Until then, I could get everything set up to make the transition to Travel, Inc. as smooth as possible.

***

I looked up from the computer screen and blinked. The sun was already setting, and the room was getting dark. I hadn't realized how much time had passed while I worked. I had been so engrossed in my laptop and making improvements that I had completely lost track of time. I quickly checked my phone, wondering if I had somehow missed Logan's call. He should have heard something back from his father by this time of day. I had honestly thought I would be a proud employee of Travel, Inc. by now.

No calls. No texts. No emails. I frowned slightly. This wasn't exactly how I had envisioned things, but then I had never been bought by a billion-dollar company before. Maybe it took more time than I thought.

"Yeah, that's it," I said to no one in particular. "These things just take time. No reason to be nervous."

I nearly jumped out of my skin when the phone started ringing, vibrating in my hands. I grinned as I recognized the number as one of the extensions of Travel, Inc.

"Hello," I said warmly into the phone. "This is Olivia Statler."

"Ms. Statler," a nasally female voice responded. "This is Mr. Logan Hayes' secretary. I regret to inform you that Travel, Inc. is no longer interested in purchasing your company."

My heart sank as I heard her words. "What!?" I frowned at the phone. There was no way I had heard that right.

"We thank you for your time and wish you the best in your endeavors. We at Travel, Inc. hope that you will continue to use Travel, Inc. for all your travel needs," she informed me.

"I don't understand. May I please speak with Logan Hayes?" I was glad I was sitting because I felt a little faint. There was no way this could be happening. There had to be some sort of misunderstanding.

"I'm sorry," the woman said. "He's unavailable at this time. Good luck, Ms. Statler." And she terminated the call.

I stared at the phone in disbelief. This couldn't be real. This had to be some sort of strange initiation joke or something. I ran to the kitchen and searched for the note he had left with his personal number. My fingers shook as I dialed it.

It rang twice. "Mr. Logan Hayes' personal line," a polite female responded. It was different than the one who had just called. She sounded nicer.

"May I please speak with Mr. Hayes? It's very important." I managed to sound professional and keep the panic out of my voice.

"Who is calling?" I could hear her typing on a computer somewhere.

"Olivia Statler," I informed her without hesitation. This had to be some sort of mistake. A funny mix-up we'd all laugh about later.

"I'm sorry, Ms. Statler," she said slowly. The typing stopped. "I've been instructed to tell you that Mr. Hayes is no longer interested in your company. Professional or private."

"I understand that," I said, even though I really didn't. This didn't make any sense. Things had gone so well yesterday! "But I really need to speak with him. It's urgent."

"I'm very sorry. That's not possible," she said firmly.

"Not possible? You're sorry?" I was getting angry now. This wasn't funny anymore. I was supposed to be sipping champagne and celebrating with Logan, not chatting with his secretaries about this nonsense. "That's not good enough. This is his private line. I want to know why he was so excited about my company yesterday and today he won't talk to me!"

The secretary was quiet for a moment. "I'm sorry, Ms. Statler. If you would like, I can transfer you to Mr. Gerald Hayes, CEO. Perhaps he can answer that question for you."

"Thank you. I would appreciate that." I rolled my eyes at her through the phone. I knew it wasn't her fault, but she wasn't making me feel any better. I did not appreciate being yanked around like this.

I heard her click a button, and hold music started

to play. I tried to take deep, calming breaths as I waited for Gerald Hayes to pick up the phone. I was furious, but I knew it wouldn't do any good to yell at the CEO of the company. I needed to be calm, cool, and professional.

"Hayes," a gravelly, masculine voice answered. It was Logan's voice, but rougher, as if he had smoked several packs of cigarettes a day for most of his life.

"Mr. Hayes, this is Olivia Statler-"

"I know who you are, Ms. Statler," he interrupted me. I wasn't phased by it.

"Well, perhaps you can explain to me why your company showed interest in acquiring my business yesterday, but today isn't even willing to let me talk to anyone?" I stood up tall in my kitchen even though I knew he couldn't see me. I felt like it would give me confidence to talk to him as an equal.

"Ms. Statler, you are confusing my son with his business. Travel, Inc. is not interested in your business nor its services. Your long-term marketing is no good, and your plan is doomed to failure. I don't invest in unsound practices, and as such, I've declined the offer," he stated. I could practically see him spinning slowly in a huge, leather chair and smoking a cigar, possibly twirling his mustache. I wanted to punch him.

"But yesterday-"

"Was yesterday," he interrupted again. "The business world moves fast, and if you aren't ready to move with it, you are going to be left behind. These are the big leagues, little girl."

I seethed a little at the implication that I was falling

behind and that he had the gall to call me a little girl.

"Now, just for the record, you gave an excellent presentation and Logan was impressed, but ultimately, he failed to impress me with what your company would do for my business. There is nothing personal here, Ms. Statler, just business," he explained.

Just business my ass, I thought. There had to be more to it than that.

"Now, I would appreciate it if you wouldn't contact us again about this matter. If our interest changes, then we'll contact you," he said. "I would also advise you to let my son be or we will be pursuing harassment charges."

"But, Mr. Hayes-"

"Goodnight, Ms. Statler," he said, then he hung up.

I stared down at the phone in disbelief yet again. I was absolutely dumbstruck. All signs had pointed to yes. What was I going to tell the other companies who'd been interested in me? I couldn't exactly call Mr. Carmichael up and say, "Hey! Just kidding about Travel, Inc.!"

I sunk to the floor as I realized it was worse than that. Word was going to spread that Travel, Inc. thought I was a bad investment, that "the long-term market was no good and your plan is doomed to failure." If the biggest and best travel company around didn't think I was a good investment, the smaller ones would have every reason to believe them. I was going to lose all my potential buyers because of this. Because I had trusted him.

A tear ran down my cheek and dropped onto the

kitchen floor. Everything was ruined. Everything I had worked so hard to achieve, my dreams of running a travel agency, of being successful, were gone. Logan had crushed them all by leading me on and making me think that he wanted me. That he had been interested not only in my business, but in me as a person.

I dialed his personal line again, but it didn't even go to the secretary. This time, I got the operator with the annoying voice telling me that the line was no longer in service.

Coward, I thought. *Doesn't even have the guts to tell me himself.* I could barely believe it. He had been so wonderful last night. I had started to let myself imagine a future with him. I had liked him so much, but now, I realized it had just been a front. He only wanted in my pants, and pretending to believe in my company was the easiest way to get there. I couldn't believe I had let myself be so easily duped.

I pulled my hair up and out of my face and took a deep breath. I wasn't about to let some coward and his terrible father make a fool of me. I had worked too hard for this.

If the Hayes family thought this was going to slow me down, they were wrong. This was just a bump in the road. My idea was a great one and it was going to work. They were going to be sorry they messed with Olivia Statler. I'd show them. I was still crying, but I'd show them all.

CHAPTER SIXTEEN

Present Day

Bang, bang, BANG!

I brought my fist down hard on the wood of Logan's hotel door. I was so angry I could barely see straight. How dare he take my employees!

He opened the door, confusion shifting into a welcoming smile as soon as he saw me. His hair was wet, and he was obviously in the middle of attempting to smooth it. Little droplets of water darkened the pale blue shoulders of his dress shirt.

"I thought I was picking you up..." he greeted me, opening the door wider to allow me in.

"What the hell is this?" I thrust the printed resignation letters into his chest. I couldn't believe he was still planning on taking me out for dinner. He fumbled with them for a moment as I crossed my arms and waited angrily for a response.

"Um..." Logan turned the sheets in his hands and did a very good job at looking legitimately confused. "They look like resignation letters? I'm afraid I don't understand what's going on."

"Like hell you don't," I sneered. "Travel, Inc. just hired four of my best consultants out from under me. What kind of sick, twisted game are you playing?"

He looked down at the papers in his hands in shock. "What?"

"What was your plan? Invite me to dinner, and while I'm distracted by your charming smile, collapse my business so you can buy it on a discount?" I took a step back into the hallway. "That's low. Even for you."

"I swear to you, I had nothing to do with this." Logan's eyes were wide and his face had lost all semblance of his earlier smile. He had his innocent act down cold. I could have almost believed him.

"*Right.* Just like you had nothing to do with it the last time you screwed me over." I took a step down the hallway, then turned as I thought of what I had always wanted to say to him. "How'd that work out for you last time?"

Logan cocked his head to the side, brows together as he stood in his doorway holding the letters. "What are you talking about?"

"The last time you did this to me." I glared up at him, fury burning through my bones. "What was the plan that time? Get my hopes up, tell my other investors off, and then wait to buy me out when I was desperate? Didn't work out so well for you. You could have had me for almost nothing. I would have given you everything. Now, I'm worth millions and not selling. This latest attempt is going to fare just as well as the first one."

"What? No, that was never..." Logan shook his head forcefully in denial. "Olivia, I had nothing to do with this! Any of it! This is all my father's doing. You have to believe me!"

"No, I don't." I gave him a cold once-over and wasn't pleased with what I saw. "I never should have believed you in the first place." I turned on my heel and marched down the hallway.

"Damn it, Olivia..." he cursed as he hurried out into the hall to follow me. "Wait, Olivia, I can explain!"

But by then, I was already to my door. I caught one last look of pleading as he ran toward me. I didn't want to hear his explanations. I had seen enough of him to last a lifetime. I didn't need to be tricked by his lying ways or my gullible heart.

It felt so good for me to slam my door in his face. I hadn't had the chance to do that the last time we had met. At least this time, Maddy wasn't here to screw things up. As I started to throw things in my suitcase, I thought about that wedding we went to a year ago.

CHAPTER SEVENTEEN

One year ago

Maddy and I sipped daintily on Cristal champagne as we wandered around the lush garden estates of our accounting firm's head partner. The soft music from a string quartet drifted among the roses as guests sipped champagne and nibbled on hors d'oeuvres while waiting for the reception to start.

The wedding of the mayor's daughter to the son of Chicago's most successful accountant was dubbed the biggest social event of the year. Everyone who was anyone was going. I hadn't known that Maddy and I were considered to be anyone until the day the invitation arrived. It felt good to be someone.

We had been invited because our accountant happened to be one of the rising stars at that particular accounting firm, as well as the fact that our little business was making waves in the travel industry. We were starting to receive recognition for our innovative approach to travel and there was no way Maddy and I were going to say no to a wedding predicted to cost well over a million dollars, even if we had no idea what to get them as a gift.

"Did you hear who is here?" Maddy whispered as we walked through an archway covered in roses.

"Who isn't here? I saw that actor you like," I whispered back. I felt like we were sneaking around the property. Despite having rented two designer dresses and getting our hair and makeup done professionally, I still felt like we didn't belong. I had this horrible premonition that security was going to find out we were there at any moment and throw us out. I had the invitation with our names on it in my purse, ready to whip out and show anyone who asked.

"I saw him, but I'm talking about Logan Hayes," Maddy said as we headed to the top of a grassy hill overlooking the main courtyard.

"I guess I'm not terribly surprised," I replied, trying to sound nonchalant. Just his name made my heart start to pound. It had been a year since I had slept with him. Not even a phone call... the bastard. He was mysteriously "out on a business trip" every time I called his office. Luckily, with Maddy around, I had moved on to other, more important things. He wasn't worth my anxiety or heartache. I was completely over him. Totally.

"I thought you hated him and were going to punch his lights out the next time you saw him?" Maddy quipped.

"Oh come on, Maddy, that was months ago," I said, waving a dismissive hand. "Eons, really."

"It was last week." She paused between two bushes covered with yellow flowers and gave me a very knowing look that I did not appreciate.

So maybe I wasn't *completely* over him.

"Okay, so maybe I still have some issues," I conceded. "But, this is a wedding. I can behave. Besides, I've had a year to cool off. He's not worth the effort of being angry. Besides, what are the odds that we'll even run into him? There are hundreds of guests here!"

"Right." Maddy gave me a skeptical look and downed the last of her champagne. "I'm going to get some more of this liquid gold goodness. You want some more?"

I held up my still mostly full glass. I didn't see what she found so special about it. It just tasted like plain old champagne to me. Dom Perignon tasted better anyway. "I'm good, thanks. I'll just wait here for you."

Maddy nodded and headed off toward the main house where the bar was set up. I sipped on my champagne again and looked out at the house and gardens. Below me in the main courtyard, the happy bride and groom were walking onto the stage. They looked so blissfully in love.

"Enjoying the champagne?" a deep voice from my dreams asked from behind me. I shivered with simultaneous want and anger. I knew that voice. I turned slowly, almost afraid that I was dreaming, but there stood Logan Hayes.

The first thing I noticed wasn't the dark blue designer suit that fit him like a glove, or the way all his hair but one stray curl was smoothed back, or even the scent of his cologne; no, it was that he looked tired. His eyes didn't have quite the luster I remembered and he looked thinner. For one whole second, I hoped he wasn't sick, but then I remembered that I'd sooner have wished him dead.

"Better than Dom," I lied. My heart was pounding like that of a petrified rabbit. I had envisioned this moment constantly for the past year, but now that it was here, I had no idea what I wanted to do. I wanted to hit him for what he did and kiss him because I wanted more. "What are you doing here?"

"I know the bride. She and I went to high school together once upon a time, and we even tried our hand at dating one another," he replied. "We decided we were much better off as friends."

"Do you know the groom, then?" I asked courteously, sipping mechanically on my champagne and trying not to panic. Slowly, though not without a fight, my anger toward him was giving way to my desire to kiss him, to run my fingers through his hair, to trace the words in his tattoo. I wanted him to not look so damn tired.

"I introduced them. Poor guy never thought he would get a girl like her, but they're perfect for each another. I get to claim matchmaker. It took a little time, but they're very happy they worked it out. It's really a sweet love story," he said with a genuinely happy smile. He stepped back and looked me up and down. "You look fantastic, by the way. Stunning, really."

"Thank you." I could be polite. I wasn't even thinking of punching him. Maddy would be shocked. "Is the rest of your family here too?"

"My brother is around here somewhere. He almost wasn't invited," he replied, glancing over toward where the music was coming from. "But Aiden knows how to apologize when he screws up. My father doesn't and as such wasn't invited."

"I'm sorry to hear that." I was secretly glad. Logan's old man could stuff it where the sun don't shine.

"Don't be. He is prone to doing things that make him very unpopular." Logan shrugged. There was a back story I knew I was missing, but I didn't want to ask. I hoped Maddy would hurry up and get back so I could leave. Being this close to him was hard. Especially when he smiled.

I sipped on my champagne and smiled politely. If this was how the rest of our interactions were going to go, I could live with that. I knew that we would be running into one another, given our similar businesses and social obligations. Maybe, if we kept having these nondescript encounters, I would forget the ache in my heart. Maybe I would stop searching for his picture in the paper every morning just to find out what he was doing. Maybe I would stop missing the something we almost had.

"I also hear that your business is taking off," he continued, taking a step closer. "I knew it would. Congratulations."

Now I wanted to punch him. He had to bring that up and rub it in. I found my anger again and hated that I had lost it for even a moment. Damn him and his stupid smile making me forget how he never called. Damn him and his father for making me scramble to save my livelihood.

"No thanks to you or Travel, Inc.," I replied with just a touch more venom than necessary.

"It was just business," he said with a frown, as if he didn't understand what my issue was with him.

"Travel, Inc.'s portion of it perhaps, but what about yours? Or did you just forget about our little car ride?" I was a little afraid I was going to crush the delicate stemware in my fist and spill champagne and glass all over the garden.

He had the good grace to blush slightly. "I wanted to apologize about that..."

"Then why didn't you?" I demanded, my temper starting to boil over. "Why did you never call me?"

"Olivia, I wanted to-- I really did-- but I couldn't," he explained. He ran a hand through his hair and dislodged another curl from his slick hairstyle. A few more passes and he would look like himself again.

"Because it is *so* hard to pick up a phone." I took a step toward him and glanced around to make sure no one was nearby. "I'm not usually that kind of girl, but I did think I at least merited a phone call. The business part I could probably have forgiven as 'just business', but the fact that you led me on is inexcusable. You let me think I was... You could have at least told me that I meant nothing to you."

He paled as my accusation hit its mark. "Olivia, it's

complicated." He started to reach out as if he wanted to touch me but thought better of it and put his hands in his pockets. "I wanted to, but my father made it very clear that I wasn't to contact you. I'm sorry."

"Unbelievable." I shook my head in disgust. "I'm so glad you do everything your father says. Do you still get an allowance for doing your homework and feeding the dog?"

"You're right. I should have called," he said softly, retreating further. "I should have done things differently."

"You're damn right you should have." I stepped back from him, wanting to put as much distance as possible between us. For all his good looks, swagger and charm, he was still a little boy under his father's influence. "You missed out on a good thing, both me and Dream Vacations."

He held me in his eyes for a moment. His expression was bleak, as if he was calculating the extent of his mistake and finding it bigger than he had first imagined. "Believe me, I know."

We stood there in silence for a moment, the two of us just staring at one another and trying to figure out how to get out of this very awkward conversation.

"Olivia, I'm back," Maddy announced, strolling up beside me and breaking the strange silence. "Who is this handsome young man you've found?"

"Maddy, this is Logan Hayes," I said flatly. "Logan, this is Maddy Sawyer, the co-owner of Dream Vacations."

"Oh my," Maddy replied with a blush. "You are

even better looking in person. I can totally see why Olivia follows you in the paper, on myFace, and won't stop talking about you."

I closed my eyes and counted to five. That was the last thing I wanted Logan to know. I wanted him to think I cared even less for him than he did for me. I didn't need him knowing he had broken my heart in just one night. "No more champagne for you, Maddy."

"Why? I'm enjoying myself," Maddy asked, puzzled. I took a big breath before I opened my eyes and glared at her. "Oh. You're *that* Logan Hayes. Travel-Inc-broke-your-heart-and-scared-off-all-your-investors Logan Hayes. Got it. Shutting up now."

Logan frowned. "What do you mean, 'broke-your-heart-and-scared-off-your-investors?'"

I purposefully ignored the first part of the question. "When word got out that Travel, Inc.'s Logan Hayes had taken me out for drinks and then dumped my business to the curb the next day, everyone thought there had to be a reason. Most of them assumed it was because you learned some terrible secret about my business. I could barely get a small business loan from the bank thanks to you." The last part was a bit of an exaggeration, but I didn't care. It got the point across.

Logan's face fell. "I had no idea. No one ever said anything to me. I'm sorry," he stammered, losing his usual calm confidence.

"Apology not accepted," I replied tartly. I was still pissed.

"Yeah," Maddy chimed in, her voice slurring. "She

still cries about it sometimes."

There was an awkward pause during which the three of us just stared at the ground for a moment. No one seemed to know what to say. The celebratory sounds of the wedding drifted up and provided a strange contrast to our uncomfortable lack of festivity. Logan was silent and then shook himself awake as if he came to some sort of conclusion in his head. Hopefully, it was to leave me alone.

"Well, it was delightful to meet you, Maddy." Logan held out his hand to shake hers. She reciprocated firmly, and pulled him in close to her.

"If you could forget the fact that I mentioned you broke Liv's heart, that would be great," she whispered, thinking I wouldn't hear. Except I could hear every cringe-inducing word. "She wouldn't want you to know that, especially because I don't think she's over you."

I was never letting her drink again. She couldn't hold onto a secret with duct tape and super glue. I half-expected her to give him my Social Security number and bank PIN while she was at it.

"Consider it forgotten," he assured her with an all-too-confident smile. I pinched the bridge of my nose, trying to convince myself that killing them both would be too much work.

Logan cleared his throat, and I looked up and into his eyes. They were big pools of brown velvet that, despite my best efforts to resist them, sucked me in. My heart pounded in my chest as I struggled to look away. He smiled, and I realized he didn't look quite as tired as he had before. "It was wonderful to see you,

Olivia. I hope to run into you again soon."

"I wish I could say the same." I plastered an obviously fake smile on my face and blinked demurely. He grinned and stepped forward, leaning in so he could whisper in my ear. Maddy's betrayal had given him back his usual cockiness in spades. He now knew he could drive me crazy, and that I wouldn't be able to stop him.

"I'll take that as a challenge," he said, his breath tickling my hair. He smelled amazing; like soap and testosterone goodness. My stomach tightened as heat surged through me. I was so mad at him, but my body craved his like a drug. Dear Lord, I had forgotten just how good he smelled. It wasn't fair that he could twist my mind and body up so easily just by standing close to me. "Someday, you'll look forward to seeing me again."

"It will be a cold day in hell," I replied sweetly, stepping back and away from his intoxicating scent. I was torn between hot lust and cold fury. He had deceived me and almost ruined my company. I had every reason to hate his stinking guts. But I found myself wanting to touch him and forgive him for everything.

His brown eyes flashed with self-assured optimism. With a polite nod to Maddy, he turned and walked down a green path toward the dance floor with the bride and groom. I stared after him, trying and failing not to check out his butt, until he disappeared into the mass of guests below.

I felt like a deflated balloon. I was still so angry and hurt by what he'd done, but for whatever reason, as soon as he got close my body forgot everything except the way he felt. It was like he had cast a spell that would cause my body to find him sexually attractive no matter what my mind thought. I understood that a ruling from his father would be difficult to break, but I had thought we had shared a connection. It couldn't have been that hard to make a single phone call? To write an email?

I chugged the last bit of my champagne. I could hear laughter coming from the wedding, but instead of feeling happy, I was jealous and bitter. I had never thought that Logan and I were going to get married or grow old together, but that night we had together was special. I had thought it was at least going to go somewhere. I never expected to be left hanging without so much as a phone call. I certainly hadn't expected it to hurt so much.

"You okay? You want mine?" Maddy asked, offering me her glass. I glanced down at my empty one and nodded. She switched glasses with me, and I chugged down the bubbly liquid.

"I hate him," I said softly, looking into the empty glass.

"No you don't," Maddy gently contradicted me. "You want to hate him. You should hate him. But, you hate that you don't hate him."

"You're drunk." I watched as she wobbled slightly on her designer heels.

"Doesn't mean I'm not right," she said with an all-too-knowing smile. "If you hated him, you wouldn't follow him on Twitter. You wouldn't know his social events, and you wouldn't blush every time someone says his name."

"I only follow him to know how to make sure I don't get caught in his web again," I explained. The champagne was finally starting to go to my head. I needed another glass. Maybe seven.

"And the blushing?" Maddy asked, eyebrows raised. It was very obvious she didn't believe me.

"He embarrassed me." I sighed and put my hand on my hip. "And I do not blush at his name."

Maddy held me in her gaze for a full beat before slowly shaking her head. "You've got some sort of torch for that man. Given the delightful way he fills out that suit, I can imagine part of it, but there's something else there." She frowned, her eyes trying to focus through the alcohol. "But you need to be careful. That man hurt you once, and I saw the aftermath of just one night with him. You can't let him do that to you again. I don't know if you'd survive a storm like Logan again."

"I have no intention of ever spending another night with that man," I said solemnly. "He may drive me crazy, but I won't let him destroy what I've worked for."

"Good." Maddy nodded emphatically. "Now, we need some more champagne. Tyler's with his grandma, neither one of us needs to drive, and there is more free booze than we can drink. Let's get our party on and get that boy out of your head!"

I glanced toward the wedding party, wondering if Logan was down there. He *was* in my head. He had sneaked in there with his charm and warm brown eyes the night I met him and, unfortunately, hadn't found his way out. I needed to forget the way his hands felt on my skin and the way he made my heart skip. It had only been one night. I should be able to forget him and move on.

A dark blue suit stepped out into an open space on the dance floor below us and I felt my heart flutter, as I recognized Logan's shape. The bride stepped into his arms with a smile and he danced with her as her husband watched, spinning her in flawless circles. She laughed and kissed his cheek as the song ended. A stab of envy hit my stomach. She had it all.

"I really need another drink," I mumbled. I wanted to forget Logan Hayes and his brown eyes and soft laugh entirely. I wanted to prove him wrong, that I would never look forward to seeing him, but I already knew I had failed.

⚜

CHAPTER EIGHTEEN

Present Day

I woke up to the sound of rain pounding against the building. There were square-shaped indentations on my cheek from having fallen asleep on my keyboard. At least I hadn't drooled, or my laptop would have been ruined. I rubbed the sleep from my eyes and groaned. Technically, I still had another five minutes before I had to get up and catch my flight, but there was no way I was going to get it. I knew I was going to want those five minutes of sleep later today. It had been a long night and was shaping up to be an even longer day.

I had been up most of the night with worry. I could feel my business and my future teetering as though on the edge of a knife. I was furious that Logan had been able to hamstring my company in four, well-paid moves. I had called each of my former employees; three had been smart enough not to pick up and the fourth apologized and promptly had an emergency to attend to.

After punching a pillow several times and threatening to stomp on my phone, I started trying to fix what I could. I posted ads for new consultants and had made some inquiries into potential applicants. I had also called my lawyer, several times. There was no way that what Travel, Inc. was doing was anywhere close to legal, but as far as getting my business on the rocks, it was effective. Mounting a legal defense would take weeks, and while Travel, Inc. would lose, the impact on my business would be big enough to force me to sell to them.

Just thinking about it was making my blood pressure rise. This was my business, and I had worked far too hard to just let them take it. I loved this company too much to give up on it now. Logan Hayes wasn't going to defeat me that easily. He may have thought his good-boy act would fool me into trusting him again, but I wasn't falling for it this time.

I slammed my laptop shut and grabbed my suitcases. I was already dressed, so one last look around the room was all it took for me to be ready. I was on my way to the lobby to get on a plane to go save my business before the light was even off.

I set my bags down in front of the check-out desk when I heard Maddy calling my name. She was hurrying toward me as fast as she could on her ankle.

"Olivia! Don't check out yet!" Maddy's cast made a hollow thunking noise as she limped over.

A ray of hope lifted my spirits. "Did the girls change their minds?" I asked with anticipation. Maybe they had come to their senses and realized what they were doing.

"No," Maddy said with a grimace. "The flight's been canceled. The tropical storm upgraded and turned South last night. We're going to have to wait out the hurricane."

Her words entered my ears, but I didn't comprehend them. I had to get home. "What?"

Maddy put a hand on my shoulder. "The island is about to be hit by a hurricane. All flights are grounded until further notice," she explained. Her brown eyes were full of sympathy as she waited for me to understand.

"But, Maddy, I have to get back-" I started but she shook her head.

"I'm sorry, Livia," she said, stopping me from saying more. "I called all the pilots I could find this morning, even the one the locals said might be crazy enough to fly through the storm. No one will do it. I'm really sorry."

My shoulders slumped as I looked from her to the big glass doors of the lobby. I had been in such a rush that I hadn't noticed that a hotel employee was busy boarding them up with plywood. The last window was blurry with rain as the final board fit into place. The empty grand entrance dimmed and echoed with muffled rain.

"What am I going to do, Maddy?" I asked as

141

desperation settled around me. I sat on my suitcase and tried to come up with a positive solution, but all I could see was the gray gloom of disaster.

"Nothing," she said softly, kneeling to meet my eyes. "There isn't anything you can do right now except go back up to your room and get some sleep. You look terrible."

I glared at her. She didn't look so hot herself.

"Well, it's true," she said in response to my angry look. "Go rest. Things won't look so bad when you're not exhausted. You've done all you can for now."

"What time is it in Chicago?" I asked, planning not to follow her advice and make more phone calls.

"Time to rest," she replied. I darkened my glare. She shrugged it off. "Your lawyer called me to ask you to stop phoning him, especially at three in the morning. He'll get back to us once he has more information."

I sighed and looked at the blockaded doors. "I just..." I whispered, losing my words to frustration.

"I know," Maddy comforted, hugging me close to her. I held onto her like a drowning person to a life-preserver.

"What are we going to do?" I whispered, feeling a tear trickle down my cheek.

"We'll come back stronger," she whispered into my ear. "This isn't the end of the world. We've faced worse and come out better because of it. Now, go rest."

She leaned back, and I nodded dejectedly. I felt like an empty balloon as I dragged my suitcases back to the elevator. I looked back at Maddy one last time before stepping through the silver doors. She gave me a weak smile and motioned me to get on.

***

The ride up was uneventful. I dropped my bags in my doorway and sank into the bed. I lay there in the dark gloom of the storm, listening to the howling of the wind and rain against the protected building. Sleep was far away and not getting any closer. There was too much to do and no way to do it. Frustration and fury writhed in my stomach like a mass of angry snakes.

I sat up. I needed to move, to vent my energy. I was up and out the door, walking the hallways before I had even made the decision to move.

The halls were dark despite the fact that it was morning. All the windows were boarded and secure, hiding most of the thin gray light from view. I wandered aimlessly from hallway to hallway, looking for a glimpse out at the storm.

The doors leading out to the garden were locked. The big window overlooking the ocean from the reception area was boarded and covered with a heavy velvet curtain. Every place I thought I might be able to look outside was boarded or locked. The sound of the wind outside was unceasing and unnerving. There was no escape. Everywhere I turned I was reminded that I was trapped here by the hurricane.

After finding yet another locked door, I growled with frustration. I couldn't even see outside, let alone change anything outside of this stupid hotel. I kicked the door and turned around in time to see Logan walk across the room at the end of the hallway. He was grinning, his hand on his bodyguard's shoulder as he laughed at something the other man said.

Rage flared red at the edges of my vision. The man who was about to ruin me was laughing. *Laughing.* Probably about me. My fingernails dug into my palms to the point of pain, but my fists just continued to tighten. The walls were closing in on me. I needed to get out. I needed to escape this nightmare.

I wrenched the doorknob of the door behind me, throwing all my weight into it. I needed to break out of the confines of the hotel. I could feel the walls pressing down on me from the weight of the wind. Logan took too much space and I needed to get as far away from him as possible. The door creaked and surprisingly gave way. It must have just been sticky, not locked.

I charged through the door and out onto the patio. The strength of the wind took me by surprise as raindrops pelted me like tiny rocks. I had seen enough reporters braving hurricanes, but that still hadn't prepared me for the raw strength of the storm. Gray waves ripped at the shoreline with furious fists of white foam while the sky churned with a dark livid power. I could suddenly understand now why no pilot had been willing to risk a flight.

I battled my way out further into the storm. The wind whipped my hair into my eyes and pulled my clothes in every direction as if to rip them from me. I could only stand in awe of the power of the storm, especially knowing that this was only the beginning.

Nature could throw more at me than this. This was just her warmup act.

I closed my eyes and let the storm surround me. I was small and insignificant in comparison to this. My problems were nothing; this wind could blow them all away with one tiny gust. In one hundred years, the elements of this storm would still exist, while my business and I would be long gone. I reached out my hands and felt the tempest inside of me raging along with the hurricane. My rage bled into the storm and released me from it.

A strong hand clamped down on my arm and forcefully spun me away from the beach.

"What are you doing?" Logan screamed at me. I stared at him for a moment in complete surprise. No one, not even me, was supposed to be out here. There was worry in his brown eyes and he was doing his best to use his broad shoulders to shield me from the wind. His hair whipped wildly around his head as his shirt darkened with rain.

"None of your business," I snapped, wrenching my arm from his grip. He was the exact person I didn't want to see. "Leave me alone!"

I took a step away from him and toward the beach. A blast of wind caught me as I left the relative safety of the patio, and I stumbled. Part of a tree whizzed down the beach, spraying pieces of leaves as it bounced like a child's ball across the sand.

Suddenly, I was up and over Logan's shoulder. He carried me as if I weighed nothing, pushing through the wind, rain, and my thrashing with ease. His shoulder was hard and warm under my stomach as his arm pinned me to him. I was furious. Furious that he was rescuing me when I didn't need saving. What I needed was to be saved from him.

I kicked and punched Logan, screaming into the storm for him to put me down. I hated that he thought he was helping me when all I wanted to do was forget about him and the trouble he was causing me. I hated him.

He opened the door to the hotel and stumbled inside. The danger of the hurricane diminished as he carried me inside the safety of the door, but my emotional fury was just getting started. He was a dead man.

CHAPTER NINETEEN

Logan set me down carefully in the hallway, dodging a well-aimed smack from me. He leaned against the door, his broad shoulders heaving as he caught his breath. I stood on shaky legs, fury pouring from every atom of my being.

"What the hell did you do that for?" I shrieked at him. I would have run back out into the storm, but he was effectively blocking the door.

"What the hell did I do that for?" he repeated, his voice incredulous. His white t-shirt was soaked with rain and clung to him like a second skin. I could see every muscle of his torso outlined in wet gray. There was what looked like grass tangled in his honey curls. He was a hot mess. A hot mess that I needed to avoid. "You were out in a fucking hurricane! Did you not see the tree hurtling down the beach?"

I glared fire at him and crossed my arms. "I was

fine! I didn't need you to come rescue me!"

Logan straightened from the door, coming to his full height. Every muscle popped out of his shirt at me, and his eyes held a dangerous darkness I had never seen before. I hadn't realized just how big he was, how strong and intimidating he could be, until that very moment.

"You ran out into a *hurricane*," he enunciated carefully. There was power and danger in his tone that gave me goosebumps. "That's how people die in these storms. What the hell were you doing out there?"

"That doesn't give you the right to pick me up like a child and carry me inside!" My voice shook with uncontrolled rage. He was close enough now that I could feel the heat radiating off his wet skin. My own hair was dripping water down my spine.

He loomed over me. There was something beautiful and dark in his eyes that held me captive and kept me from running. "Damn it, Olivia!" Logan growled. Frustration reverberated off every syllable. "I was worried about you!"

"Why?" I asked with a sneer. "If I got killed out there, you would get my company for a song. No more Olivia problem. You already have most of my employees anyway."

"I had nothing to do with that!" he shouted, anger making his voice break. "I haven't done jack shit to your company!"

"Liar," I hissed, narrowing my eyes. He stepped back as if I had struck him. He took a deep breath, visibly trying to calm himself.

"Everything you hate was done by my father. I don't want your company." His brown eyes were flames, and my soul was the moth. I couldn't have escaped from his gaze if I had been blinded. He moved close enough that those eyes were all I could see. "I want you."

I blinked twice. That was not what I was expecting. His words startled and excited me, but before my brain could analyze and process them, his hand was around the back of my neck and his lips were on mine.

His mouth was hot and insistent as he pressed it against mine. I fought for a moment, but his grip was too strong and his kiss too sweet. It was a kiss I had craved for two years and had tried to convince myself I could do without. I wanted to give in to him completely, but I was still too angry to budge even an inch. Instead, I just stood there like a statue as he kissed me. I was furious and turned on beyond anything I could imagine. After a moment, he pulled back and searched my face.

"What was that for?" I surprised myself with the amount of venom in my voice. His kiss had sent want scorching down into the very marrow of my bones, but I needed someone to be angry with, and he was the closest person. He had hurt me. His eyebrows came together above those beautiful eyes. Hope fell as he saw something in my expression that disappointed him.

"Forget it," he mumbled, releasing me and looking away. His shoulders hunched and he moved to leave, but I wasn't about to let him get away that easily. He couldn't kiss me like that and just run away without an explanation. I grabbed his shoulder and spun him back to face me. He frowned, his brown eyes filling with heartbreak. I looked deeper, trying to understand what was going on. Passion and something sweet burned deep within their coffee and caramel swirls. The black of his pupils threatened to suck me into their depths and made my heart melt and core heat. His kiss had awakened a deep need, and my body was responding without letting my brain get a say in things.

Without thinking, I put my hand on the back of his neck and pressed my mouth into his. He didn't hesitate, kissing me back with a need that matched my own. He pushed me up against the wall. Our tongues interlocked as we found the valve for the sexual tension that had been building between the two of us for the past two years. My body responded to his every touch with a fervor I couldn't contain. Didn't want to contain. I wanted it to consume us both.

Logan's grip tightened around my waist, drawing me in to him. I arched my hips, wanting to press every inch of my body to his. His body was hard, hot, and responding to mine in the most obvious of ways. I was sure steam was coming off both of our wet clothes with the heat we were generating. My fingers tightened into his golden curls, squeezing water out of them as I held him greedily closer to me. He tasted so good, I was sure I would never get enough.

Logan wasn't holding back. One hand threaded into my hair and he tangled my wet tresses around his fingers. The other cupped my breast through my soaked shirt. Everything in my world was lost to necessity. I needed Logan more than anything I could possibly think of.

As if on cue, we both broke apart for a moment, gasping for air like we had both forgotten how to breathe. To be honest, I couldn't remember breathing before our kiss. His lips had stolen all of my brain power, and I was surprised that my heart had managed to beat on its own without my brain supplying the stimulus. I thanked God for autonomic functions.

I stared up into his fathomless brown eyes. Gold swirls and amber highlights pulled me ever deeper into his soul. All that I could see was his warmth and desire. It terrified me because I knew I was reflecting the same things. I wanted him. I had wanted him for the past two years and had almost convinced myself that I didn't.

I thought of bolting. There was too much emotion, too much history, and too much baggage to even be thinking of kissing him again. But I wanted to kiss him again. I wanted to do so much more than just kiss him. Everything about our relationship was wrong. But everything in my body was telling me that this was right. That *we* were right. That we had always been right, and that I had been doing my damnedest not to see it.

"Logan?" I whispered. The storm and my own heartbeat were the only things I could hear. It felt like the hurricane was still raging around and through me. I loved him and hated him. I wanted this so badly, yet I knew I should run. I was shaking under his hands as

I tried desperately to sort out my emotions and come up with a plan. If I had a plan, then I could be rational. I wouldn't get hurt again.

His face was unreadable as he searched mine. I wanted him to push me away and hold me close at the same time. My conflicting emotions and thoughts spun around me like raindrops in the wind. I had hated him for so long. The realization that I actually wanted him instead was still a foreign idea. It wasn't anywhere close to my usually rational self, and that frightened me.

He brushed a strand of wet hair from my cheek. His touch was tender and full of a soft caring that made my heart ache. He had just walked into a hurricane because he cared for me. He wanted me, not just physically, but emotionally too. No one would walk out into a hurricane for just a one-night stand. My throat clenched, afraid of what might come out of his mouth. I tightened my grip on his wet shirt, afraid he would tell me exactly what I wanted to hear.

"Olivia..." It was only one word, but when he said my name, it was the equivalent of a full conversation. It was all the "I'm sorry" that needed to be said. The "it's not your fault," the "I'll fix it," and "I need you." It was everything I wanted to hear him say all wrapped up in my name.

He dipped his head and kissed me again. Pure need overwhelmed the uncertainty and chaos in my mind. I wanted him. I needed to be with him, to have him all for myself. All thoughts of business, history, and reason left and all that remained was my pure desire. I didn't need to be rational. Lust pulsed with a white-hot heat in the middle of my belly. He was the only thing that mattered.

"Yours or mine?" I gasped, pressing my hips up against his. I could feel his need matching mine.

Logan glanced down the hallway, mentally calculating the distances between the closest elevators and each of our rooms. "Mine's closer."

I nodded, and he grabbed my hand. The two of us sprinted toward the secondary elevator doors that let out by his room. The pleasant ding of the elevator greeted us as we rushed in and hit the button for the third floor.

I was kissing him again the instant the metallic doors slid shut. He tasted like rain, and I couldn't get enough. His hands caressed my body, hot against the cold of my rain-soaked clothes. His every movement was wrought with passion, and I lost myself to his grasping, groping fingers.

My leg wrapped around him of its own accord. I wanted him right then and there in the elevator with our bodies, naked and wet, pressed against the mirrored surface of the elevator's interior. The idea sent heat rushing through me, and I tightened my leg around him. His hands traveled up under my shirt, his palms hot against the damp skin of my ribs.

Someone cleared his throat, startling me out of my reverie. The elevator doors had opened without our knowing it. Two men were staring at us. I recognized them from one of the other travel agencies visiting the resort. The taller of the two cocked an eyebrow at the erotic tableau Logan and I were presenting.

I dropped my leg and scurried out of the elevator,

KRISTA LAKES

feeling my cheeks reddening in pure embarrassment. Logan was right behind me as we exchanged places with the other guests.

"You two have fun now!" One of the two men called out after us. I didn't have the fortitude to look back and see who it had had been. The heat in my cheeks increased. Logan laughed, though he seemed just as anxious as I was to disappear from their view.

As soon as we were free from their stares, I was back in his arms. The hallway was deserted, which was good, because I couldn't stop kissing him. His kisses grew rougher and more demanding the closer we got to his door. We weaved across the hallway like we were drunk as we made out. He pushed me up against the door to his hotel room, one hand pulling me into him while the other fumbled with his key-card.

I gently tugged on his earlobe with my teeth, arching my hips up and into his groin. Logan missed the slot for his key-card by a mile. He cursed softly, his breath tickling the sensitive skin on my neck. I loved that I had that effect on him.

I heard the lock click as he got the key into the slot, and together we tumbled into the room. Logan pushed me up against the wall as the door slammed shut behind us. His strong hands found my wrists and pinned them above my head while his lips found the hollow of my neck and jaw. I whimpered, completely at his mercy.

His tongue skimmed my jawline and up to my ear. "Say it," he whispered.

I wanted to resist him, but my mouth couldn't find

the words to tell him no. Longing pounded and pulsed through every nerve in my body. I could barely breathe for the pure desire choking me.

"I want you," I gasped. "So much. Too much."

This wasn't going to give us a happily-ever-after. This was a mistake and the rational part of me knew it, but I didn't care. I could have him again. He could be mine for a night, just this once more. His touch had haunted my dreams for two years and I was finally going to experience it again. The sensible part of my brain gave up trying to fight. The physical energy and connection between us was too strong. Maybe by giving into him, I could finally forget. Maybe this wouldn't live up to the memory I held close to my heart.

Maybe. But so far, it was even better than I remembered.

I could feel him smile against my skin as he dragged his teeth along my shoulder and kissed his way down the collar of my shirt. Goosebumps popped up all over my skin. He nibbled at my collarbone, making me hum with pleasure.

Leaving one hand to keep my wrists pinned to the wall, he dropped the other and slid it up my shirt. He caressed the soft swell of my breast and I could almost feel his touch through the lacy fabric of my bra. My nipple hardened against the fabric as if it was trying to reach him. An eager moan escaped my lips.

He let go of my wrists, using the freed hand to rip the wet shirt from my body. His pupils dilated as he looked down at the bare skin of my chest peeking through the lace of my exposed bra. He licked his lips and leaned forward to kiss the edges of my bared skin. My brain, and whatever was left of rational thought, melted out of my ears.

I grabbed at his shirt, finally peeling it off his back and over his head. He kissed me, pressing our chests together. Our skin was sticky from the rain. It was cold and hot at the same time. Reaching one clever hand around me, he deftly unclasped my bra and pulled it out from between us.

Heat flooded through me as every inch of my chest pressed into his solid muscles. I could feel his delicious hardness growing against my thigh. My body ached to have him inside of me. I could barely think of anything else. I needed him to join with me and ease the terrible void he had left for two years.

I slid out of my shoes, kicking them to the side as I wiggled out of my pants. Logan stepped back to watch as I stood before him, wearing nothing but a skimpy purple thong. His pupils dilated again as he took in the view and his mouth opened slightly. After a moment, he shook his head as if to clear his thoughts, then kicked off his own shoes.

He towered over me, looking dark, dangerous, and completely sexy. All my doubt, all the fear and reluctance to put myself in his power again, was burned away by the sheer desire covering his face. He craved me like a drug. Had he yearned for me over these past two years? The idea came unbidden and seemed impossible. I shoved it aside for later. With him standing there, looking powerful and hungry as hell, there was no way I was going to say no.

My fingers were on the button to his shorts before

I even had to think about it. He groaned slightly as I freed him from the restriction of his clothing. His shorts fell to the floor, and he stepped out of them. His dark blue boxer-briefs strained at the seams to control his manhood.

He dropped slowly to his knees in front of me, and I rested my fingertips on the muscles of his broad shoulders. He looked up at me, dark eyes burning, as he slowly took my breast in his mouth. I gasped as he surrounded the pink nub of my nipple with warmth. He kissed the soft flesh, nipping gently, making me arch my back and moan.

His strong hands slid up my legs. From calf to thigh to hip, no inch of skin was left unexplored by his hands. His fingers danced along the tiny purple triangle of fabric covering my front. Electricity skittered from his touch and flashed up my spine like lightning. I couldn't help but shiver as pure lust surged through my system.

He chuckled at my visceral reaction to his touch, his voice muffled by my chest. He had shaved that morning, so his cheeks were mostly smooth against my skin. I remembered how much I had enjoyed his fresh shave last time, too. He bit down gently on a nipple, just hard enough for me to cry out and rake my fingers through his hair.

Slowly, he pushed the fabric of my panties to the side and ran his thumb along the newly exposed flesh. I whimpered, leaning into the wall as he proceeded to find ways to make my knees go weak. It took him no time at all to find my engorged nub and begin stroking it like an instrument.

KRISTA LAKES

He played my body like an expert musician, making me hum and cry out as his fingers deftly explored my pleasure. White heat of ecstatic lightning flashed through me, flooding every sense with pure rapture. My hips bucked against his fingers while his mouth kept pleasuring my breasts. My knees buckled as I gave into the pleasure, my body vibrating as a tidal wave of orgasm flowed through me.

I would have collapsed to the floor if Logan hadn't wrapped his arm around my waist and held me up. He supported me easily until my strength returned. I realized my fingers were still tangled in his honey curls and that I had probably nearly ripped them out of his head with the strength of my orgasm. He grinned up at me, inching the thong down my thighs. I shimmied out of it as he stood to his full height.

He kissed me again, powerful and primal. I pushed my hips into his groin, feeling his hardness yearning to escape its cloth prison. Having him inside of me was all I could think about. I pulled the briefs down and caressed his silky length.

A low, masculine sound of longing tumbled from his lips as I touched him. He was velvet over steel. Our eyes locked and I nodded. He pressed his lips against mine for a brief moment before reaching for his shorts. In no time, he found the condom in his wallet and put it on as I watched with eager appreciation. He was so damn sexy. I couldn't believe how much I wanted him.

Placing his hands on my hips, he lifted me effortlessly, though the muscles in his arms flexed with the motion. My legs wrapped around his waist and slowly-- so slowly I wanted to scream-- he lowered me onto him.

Our twin gasps of pleasure echoed through the room. The sensation of being filled to the brink was the only thing in my world that mattered. At last we were one. He pushed my back against the wall as he palmed my ass. I rocked into him, but he set the beat. Each thrust sent me to new heights. His hips moved back and forth as I rocked into him. I wrapped my hands against the bulge of his biceps. His muscles were rigid and strong. His amazingly sexy grunts weren't from overexertion; they were from sheer pleasure.

"More," I gasped, yet the word was insufficient for what I needed. I wanted him. I wanted every inch of him in me and on me. An out-of-control storm of desire raged within me that put the hurricane outside to shame.

"Oh, God, Olivia," he groaned as I arched my hips, coaxing his shaft deeper. He buried his face into my shoulder and thrust up harder. I cried out, begging for more. He pulled away from the wall and walked, with me skewered to him, over to the bed. With an easy lift, he tossed me onto the mattress.

Pillows went flying. I stared up at him, marveling at his delicious length. I spread my legs, offering myself up to him. He growled and jumped on top of me. He found my opening and dove in, thrusting deeper than I thought I could take.

Writhing like a snake, I arched and danced against him. His skin was still damp from the rain, and I reveled in the way we stuck together. He slammed into me, his passion driving me insane. I wanted him harder and faster. I wanted us to crest into oblivion together, but at the same time I was desperate for this never to end. I bent my knees, giving him every angle to drive as deep as possible.

"Olivia," he gasped, his voice rough and thick. I looked up into his eyes, and my world exploded. Together we dove into oblivion, losing ourselves to one another and the storm raging within us. I felt a cry of ecstasy reverberate through my entire being as we merged and fell together. His body tensed and relaxed against mine. I lost myself to him, reveling in the low, male sound of his gratification.

Slowly, the colors of the room stopped flashing before my eyes, and I could see again. I hadn't felt pleasure like that in a long time. Just over two years, actually. No one had been able to make me feel the way Logan did. It was as if he was the secret key to pleasuring my body.

I stared into Logan's eyes. He smiled and kissed the tip of my nose. The lust still burned bright in him, but with this release, I could see there was more than just desire. He wasn't going to ask me to leave. If anything, he wanted me to stay. He didn't want this to only be a one-time thing. I was surprised to find that I didn't either.

As our breathing slowed from frantic to fast, I wondered what was going to happen next. Was this just something that we needed to get out of our systems, or did we have a chance? I wanted to believe that this wasn't just sexual tension finally breaking free. I wanted to believe the promise in his eyes that he truly cared.

The wind and rain howled at the windows, threatening destruction, but wrapped up in Logan's arms, I felt safe. For the first time in two years, I felt the storm inside of me settling down.

CHAPTER TWENTY

Rain pulsed against the window like the heart of a living creature. I could imagine that there was nothing outside of this room but a monster of rain and wind. I reveled in the idea of spending eternity like this, trapped with Logan in the pit of the monster's stomach where no one could find us.

Logan's long fingers traced the curve of my spine as I closed my eyes and focused on his touch. I lay on my front, bedsheets tangled around my feet as he sat beside me, admiring my skin. I couldn't remember feeling this satiated or relaxed in forever.

"God, you are so beautiful," he whispered. The compliment made me blush with pleasure. Logan's lips caressed my shoulder, his kiss soft and appreciative.

I rolled over, propping my head on my hand to look at him. I smiled. Based entirely on the way he was looking at me, I believed him. His eyes held so much life and emotion, I was sure I would drown in them. I was torn between languid happiness and shock that I had allowed this to happen. Once again, I had given in to my desires and let my body overrule my mind. I could feel the edge of regret creeping up, but I pushed it away, wishing to stay in this moment a little longer.

I stared openly at him, memorizing the way he looked so I could keep this image stored away for a lonely night. The sheet covered his bottom half, but just barely. His broad shoulders tightened down to muscled abs, and the top of his hip poked out from under the sheet, proving he was naked underneath. His tattoo was exactly the way I remembered it. I skimmed his skin with my eyes, knowing that I could look as much as I wanted to. It had felt so good to finally touch him and give my body what it wanted.

"You know," I said slowly, never taking my eyes off of him, "I'm still mad at you." It was hard to feel angry, though, when I felt this good.

He raised his eyebrows and ran a hand through his disheveled hair. I loved the way those honey-colored curls had tangled around my fingers just moments before. I shifted slightly in the bed, already feeling sore in all the right places.

Regret was creeping in as I regained my senses. I stubbornly ignored it; I didn't want to feel regret yet. Anger I could handle, but I had enough regret to last a lifetime. "I'm still not exactly sure how this happened," I said softly.

Knowing I was referring to the mess we'd made of

his room, Logan glanced around. Clothes dangled haphazardly from the furniture, and a chair had been overturned in our haste to get to the bed, which was in itself a disaster. Sheets were tangled between our bodies, the comforter hung off the bed, and the fitted sheet was nowhere to be seen. Pillows lay scattered around the bed and floor as if there had been an explosion, and I supposed in a way there had been. The maid was going to wonder what kind of animals had gotten into Logan's room.

"You finally gave into my charms." Logan's eyes heated for a moment as he remembered the delectable details. "They were bound to get you eventually."

I gave his arm a playful smack. "Your charms? I was trying very hard to avoid you."

He leaned forward and nuzzled the tender skin just below my ear, making my breath catch with sudden desire. Two minutes ago, I had been so blissfully worn-out that I was sure I was never going to move again, but with just the trace of his kiss on my neck, I was ready for more. Charms, indeed.

"Why would you want to avoid me?" he whispered, his kisses working down the curve of my shoulder. His brown eyes looked up at me as he gave me one last affectionate peck.

"Because you're kind of a jerk," I informed him. He frowned, pulling back slightly. "You hurt me pretty badly the last time we were together."

"But that wasn't my fault," he said quietly, innocently. "I told you that."

I sighed. Logan had grown up in a world with

almost no repercussions as long as his father was pleased. I didn't think he even realized the full extent of what he had cost me. "Doesn't change the fact that it still hurt." I bit my lip and looked him in the eye, watching his every move. "I need to know: are you going to hurt me again?"

Pain and remorse flashed across his face and he reached out and stroked my cheek. His touch was soft and gentle. "I'm never going to hurt you again. I promise."

I liked the way those words sounded, but I had been burned too badly to fully believe them. I would have to see them proven, not just hear them spoken. I smiled despite my hesitation. For this moment in time, they would be enough. "What happened last time anyway?"

"Which part do you want first?" he asked, sliding down on the bed to lay facing me.

"Business," I decided. I could handle that part better. "You had me believing you were going to buy me out."

"I was," he stated, brushing a strand of hair behind my ear. "Even before I met you, I thought your idea was amazing. I knew Dream Vacations would be an invaluable asset the moment I learned about your program."

"Then what happened?"

He looked down for a moment. "I oversold it. My brother pointed out that I was trying too hard to convince Dad, and I probably was. I should have just let him see the initial proposal and not personally endorsed it. I certainly should have waited on drinks, too."

"What do you mean?" I asked, confused. "Why would your endorsement or getting drinks with me change things?"

"My father has made some poor business decisions with regard to women." His mouth twisted into a parody of a smile that implied it'd been far worse. "He cost the business millions before my brother and I took over negotiations and acquisitions. Dad almost bankrupted us because of a pretty face, yet he still gets to make the final call. I think my brother assumed I was following in my father's footsteps when I pushed so hard for your company."

"Were you?" I held my breath waiting for the answer.

Logan's eyes met mine, serious and honest. "Your company was sound. I would have wanted Dream Vacations even if you were a balding eighty-year-old man." He paused and smiled. "I just wouldn't have bought you drinks."

"So, your father turned down my proposal because he thought you were just trying to get laid? That I was some sort of gold-digger?" It definitely wasn't the reason I was expecting.

"Yes. And all my attempts to convince him of the contrary just worried him further," Logan explained. "Once he saw himself in my actions, he wouldn't let it go."

"You fought for me?" I asked quietly, gratitude blooming in my stomach. He hadn't just left me to rot like I had thought. He had tried to convince his father to change his mind. His explanation rang true with what I knew of his father; I had heard enough of Gerald Hayes' rumors to completely believe Logan's story. It would even begin explain why Gerald had cut off our communication. He thought he was protecting his son from me.

"Too much, according to him." Logan nodded and gave me a wry smile. "I have to admit, it's been great watching you succeed on your own and getting to rub his face in it."

"Anytime." I smiled and he kissed my forehead. He had defended me. The thought made me melt inside. "So why does your father want my company now? What changed?"

"Your success. The board of directors is pushing him to get you on board. Concierge travel is the future and he missed his opportunity to get in on the ground floor because he didn't believe in me." Logan shrugged. "Now, he'll do anything to fix his mistake. Otherwise, the board of directors will destroy him. As the COO, I am required to help him."

"Ah, I see." I nodded. At least I knew now that Logan wasn't out to get me and why he kept sending me acquisition offers. I was now ready to hear the other half of the story. "So, then, why didn't you call me?"

A shadow passed over Logan's features. "Dad made it very clear that he would make my life a living hell if I did. My personal phone line mysteriously went down, and he sent me on a business trip to Malaysia that next day. He made his threat clear. He kept me there for three months working crazy hours."

I frowned. All of that sounded terrible, but he was

a billionaire. There had still been ways to contact me. I tried to hide the disappointment that I had apparently meant less to him than he had to me.

"I tried to call you," he said softly. "I called you from the hotel once, but I didn't know what to say so I hung up as soon as you answered. I thought maybe a quick, clean break before we got in too deep would be easier for you. That the feelings were all on my end and you would move onto someone else."

I remembered that midnight call. I had woken up dreaming that it was Logan calling, only to hear silence on the other line. "I was in too deep the moment I agreed to drinks," I confessed. "I don't think there was an easy way to let me down after that."

He ran his fingers along my cheek. I closed my eyes and leaned into his touch. "I wanted you to be mine as soon as I saw you. Until I saw you at that wedding, I didn't think I stood a chance after what I did. I can't tell you how much I appreciated Maddy being drunk."

I laughed. "I was so ready to kill her for that."

"I'm sorry I hurt you." He kissed the tip of my nose, and I opened my eyes to look at him. He was so damn handsome that it made my heart hurt. This had to be a dream. Not only was I with the man I couldn't forget, but we were working things out.

I shrugged slightly. "I'm working on forgiving you."

He leaned forward and kissed me again. His lips were sweet and sent small thrills down my spine. It blew my mind how well the man could kiss. He pulled back and examined the results of his work. "How am I doing?"

"Good." Words were hard to come up with after a kiss like that. "Really…good."

He chuckled. "I'll get you there eventually."

"What about your dad?" I asked. The thought hit me like a blow to the stomach. He had already nearly ruined me once and was on track to do so again. "I can't imagine he'd be thrilled about me in your bed, especially given how he lured my employees away from me."

"Let me worry about my father. Right now, this isn't business. This is us." He touched my cheek again, forming a connection between us once more. I never wanted him to stop touching me. "My father has an excellent mind for business, or at least he used to. However, when it comes to his children, he is stubborn and usually wrong."

"I'm sorry," I said softly, not knowing how else I could respond.

"He's still my dad, and I of course love him." He shrugged and fell away from me onto his back. His eyes focused on the ceiling, seeing memories instead of wood. "I think when mom died, he just lost the part of him that knew how to feel. His heart died with her. He buried himself in his business. My brother and I… I think we remind him of her, so he just chooses to view us as employees rather than family. It's easier for him that way."

His voice ached with a quiet, secret sorrow. To lose a mother, and then have your father retreat because of it would be terrible. I kissed his cheek, feeling a slight prickle against my lips. "That sounds terrible."

"Mom died when I was ten. I remember my dad as a totally different person. He never would have pulled this crap with your company when Mom was around. She was, in a lot of ways, his conscience. When she left us, she took the best part of him with her." He took a deep breath and let it out slowly. "I kept thinking that if I just showed him how good Aiden and I could be, he would be his old self again. But, after welcoming three gold-digging step-mothers, graduating top of my class, perfect business records, and doing everything he has ever asked of me, nothing has changed."

I lifted his arm and tucked it around me so I could rest my head in the hollow of his shoulder. He pulled me close to him, as if he needed to hold onto me. Logan's attempts to impress his father made a strange sort of logic. He just wanted the father he had once had and was trying his best to make it happen. "You know it's not your fault, right? You can't change him. Only he can do that."

"I know. I'm thirty-two years old, yet I only recently realized I was still behaving like a ten-year-old boy seeking my father's approval instead of finding my own way." He sighed somewhat shakily. "I've done everything in my power to make him happy, but he never changes. He never will."

I squeezed my eyes shut and nestled in to him. This was a side of Logan Hayes that no one ever got to see. I should know. I'd practically stalked him online. But here, with me, he was vulnerable and lost.

He was struggling like the rest of us mortals to come to terms with his place in the world. I liked seeing this human side of him, even though his pain broke my heart. "I wish I could take your pain away," I whispered.

He tightened his arm around me and then raised one hand to tip my chin up so that we were looking into one another's faces. "You already have." His eyes were warm and full of complete sincerity. He smiled softly, and I realized that he legitimately liked me. Maybe even loved me. Joy surged through me as if I'd been asked to prom by my high-school crush. "You make me happier than I've been in a long time."

"You really are as charming as you appear, aren't you?" I purred, falling into the dark velvet of his eyes. Between those eyes and that smile, I was never going to escape his allure. I didn't want to.

"Probably," he replied, his grin gaining a touch of cockiness. "It just depends on how charming you think I am."

"Very." So much so that I was willing to make the same mistakes over and over again just to see that smile. I was a lovestruck idiot.

"Good. I have to keep you somehow," he murmured, moving to kiss me on the top of my head.

This was a beautiful moment, so of course I had to ruin it. My stomach rumbled. It was loud enough to be audible even over the constant roar of the storm.

"Sorry." I couldn't believe it had been that loud. Logan laughed, his chest reverberating mirthfully against my shoulder.

"I guess you're hungry," he teased. "Let's get some

food. I was told they're still delivering room service even though it's storming."

"Really? That sounds wonderful. I'm starving, but I don't want to get up." I glanced down at my watch. "Holy cow. It's two in the afternoon."

"Already? Time flies when you're having fun," Logan mused, slowly sitting up. He looked around until he saw the room service menu on the far desk. I lost my breath as he stood. His toned, naked body displayed its perfection to me. I couldn't take my eyes off him as he sauntered to the desk and retrieved the menus, completely unaware of the effect he was having on my lady parts.

I quickly tried to remember if I had anything planned for this evening, or if I could stay here and continue having more fun. I would have to check my phone, which was in my pants across the room, and I had no intention of leaving this bed unless it was for food.

"Maddy must be wondering where I am," I mused out loud. I hoped she just thought I was napping.

"I won't tell if you don't," Logan replied, sitting down on the edge of the bed and handing me a menu. "I'm not sure she likes me all that much."

"She's just being protective of me, and until you explained everything, she had good reason," I told him. "She's kind of a best friend, guard dog, mom and secretary all rolled into one smart lady."

"She doesn't have to worry. I wouldn't hurt you for the world. And, I can't tell you how sorry I am for the last time." His face grew serious. "I knew then just how amazing you were, and I should have called you that morning and never stopped. My father and his company be damned."

"You already got me into your bed. You don't have to keep charming me," I said with a smile. He relaxed his shoulders and grinned.

"Maybe I want more than you just in my bed."

I looked up from the menu with wide eyes. Did he mean what I thought he meant? I didn't think we were quite at the point of talking about the future yet. While we were connecting fantastically, we'd only been together for under a day. Furthermore, most of that time had been physical, and we both knew our sexual chemistry had a far better track record than our emotional one.

"I mean," he explained smoothly, as if he had always meant to continue his sentence, "I'm hoping to get some of your food. Other people's fries always taste better."

He flashed a friendly smile before looking down to continue perusing his menu. I couldn't be sure, but I had a strong feeling that he hadn't really been talking about French fries. I wondered if he had been keeping tabs on me like I had kept tabs on him. No matter how many times I cleared my history, his name was my favorite Google search term. I knew there was only a hair's width of difference between love and hate and that I swung wildly around him.

"I'm going to get the Maui burger," Logan announced, setting the menu down. "What about you?"

"I'll get a cobb salad," I answered. "You're getting the burger with pineapple on it? Gross."

"Not gross. Delicious. Besides, you're getting a salad. On vacation." His disgust at my healthy choice was obvious, and his skeptical frown made me laugh.

"It's got bacon. And eggs." I handed him my menu.

"It's a *salad*." He took my menu but didn't pick up the phone, giving me a chance to change my mind before he ordered.

"I happen to like salads," I said, sticking my tongue out at him.

"I happen to like you," he responded immediately. A little blush colored my cheeks. What a flirt he was. "Still, a salad?"

"You're right. It's vacation. Get me the brownie sundae for dessert," I acquiesced.

"That's more like it," he said with a grin.

While he picked up the phone and ordered, I stretched out on the bed, feeling the sheets slide across my skin as his voice caressed my ears. I felt wonderful. Being with Logan, tangled up in sheets felt luxurious and comfortable at the same time. Being with him like this, now that I didn't think he was out to get me, was easy. Almost too easy.

"They'll be here in thirty minutes," Logan informed me, hanging up the phone.

"Thirty minutes?" I whined. I was hungry now. "I don't know if I'll last that long."

A naughty smirk lit up Logan's features. "I guess I'll just have to distract you until then."

I trembled at his words, feeling a different kind of hunger fill me. A hunger that only Logan could satisfy.

"Distract away," I said, my voice breathless with want. Logan's eyes darkened and his body hardened as he bent over me and began to make me crave only his body.

CHAPTER TWENTY-ONE

"You go on in," I told Logan as I entered the password into my phone. "I'll be right there."

"Okay," he murmured into my hair, kissing me before heading toward the bathroom. I raised my eyes from the screen to watch his muscled ass as he walked. I bit my bottom lip and made a little noise of appreciation when he leaned over to turn on the shower. He must have heard me, because he turned and winked at me before stepping into the spray of water. I was sad when he closed the glass door,blurring my view of water sluicing down his body.

I had two missed calls and a bunch of emails. The messages could wait until later, but I needed to call Maddy and assure her that I wasn't dead.

"Hey, Maddy," I greeted her when she picked up the phone on the third ring. "You called?"

"I checked your room to see if you wanted some dinner, and you weren't there." I could hear the TV on in the background. She must have been in her room. "You doing okay?"

"Yeah, I'm fine. I'm actually feeling better about things." Logan's administrations had me feeling more than fine, but I wasn't ready to tell her about him yet. She wasn't Logan's biggest admirer, and I knew she would discourage me from seeing him. But right now, he was the only person I wanted to see.

"Good!" I could hear the smile in her voice. "You want to come to dinner with Tyler and me? There is a very good chance, though, that Tyler will go see the dog and ditch me. I could use the company."

"Thanks," I said slowly. I could see the hazy outline of Logan's body in the shower. I really wanted to get wet with him. "But I can't. You two have some good mother-son-dog bonding time without me. Go with him to feed the dog or something."

"Because that's my idea of a great vacation." Maddy's eye-rolling was audible.

"I wanted to ask, how is Spock doing? Tyler did a great job of setting things up for him." I watched through the glass as Logan soaped himself up. The tempered glass door hid the details, but my imagination was doing a fantastic job of adding them in.

"The dog doesn't like the room, but other than that he's doing well. Tyler's planning on sleeping with him down there tonight," Maddy said. I knew her well enough to tell she was shaking her head at the thought. "I don't know how I'm going to tell him the dog can't come home with us."

"Are you sure about that, Maddy?" I hesitated to say it was a bad idea, but I knew I was going to have to help Tyler sell the dog to her. "Tyler's such a good kid. He deserves a friend."

"You've made a friend here, too, haven't you?" Maddy asked, changing the subject and catching me off guard.

"What? I haven't found a dog..." I really hoped she didn't know about Logan.

"Disappearing all day and now sounding all happy and content? Please. There are some definite hotties around here," she said, trying to sound nonchalant and failing miserably. She was living vicariously through me. "That surfing instructor was pretty easy on the eyes. Please tell me it's the surfing instructor."

"Maddy, I have no idea what you're talking about." That was only a little lie. I didn't know who the surfing instructor was.

"Fine," she pouted. "Just know that I'm a little jealous, but I'm glad you're finally finding a way to relax. How about I see you for lunch tomorrow? You can tell me all about his perfect six-pack abs then."

I couldn't help but smile. "Sounds good. I'll see you then."

"Oh, and one more thing," she added quickly. "Stay away from Logan Hayes. You don't need him complicating things or messing with your head any more than he already has. That man's trouble."

"I'll keep that in mind," I replied, hoping I wasn't giving everything away with my voice. Maddy had the ability to see right through me when she wanted to.

"Okay. Have fun, and I'll see you tomorrow."

"Bye, Maddy." I clicked the phone off and tossed it onto the bed. I was about to disregard Maddy's recommendation-- hell, I already had. That shower had waited long enough.

CHAPTER TWENTY-TWO

Gray light seeped through the edges of the boarded-up window, but instead of making Logan's room seem gloomy, it simply made me sleepy. I guessed it must still be early morning, but with the storm hiding the sun, it was difficult to tell. A gust of wind shook the boards on the windows, but they were locked down tight. So far, the hotel had withstood the force of the hurricane as if it were nothing more than a summer breeze. Noah had done a good job.

I rolled to my side, expecting to find a warm body to cuddle up against. Instead, I found empty sheets. The space was cold. Logan was long gone from the bed. A moment of panic washed over me, but peeking out through the doorway, I could see the glow of a computer screen in the other room. I instantly relaxed. He was just working. I could understand that. The man ran a multibillion-dollar travel company; he had to work sometime.

I reached out to the nightstand and checked my smartphone. It was only a little after eight in the morning, but the little blinking alert light was going crazy. In addition to all the emails I'd ignored previously, I'd received five urgent messages. I hoped, maybe, that one or two of them might be my consultants asking to return to Dream Vacations, or maybe my lawyer telling me I'd be able to destroy Gerald Hayes in court. Either way, I needed to go to my room and use my computer.

I slid silently out of bed and tiptoed out to the living area. Logan's room was similar to mine. He sat typing away at the work desk. I crept up behind him, grinning like a naughty school girl at the thrill of startling him. It looked like he was emailing someone, but I did my best not to read over his shoulder.

"Good morning, handsome," I whispered seductively in his ear.

Logan jumped practically three feet into the air and slammed the laptop shut. I giggled and came to sit on his lap. He stared at me for a moment, his hand still pressing down on his computer.

"Good morning to you too," he finally spit out. There was an edge to his words that I wasn't expecting, but I put it off as just being annoyed that I had scared him. He quickly shuffled the papers laying on the desk into a computer bag and out of sight. It was almost as if he didn't want me to see them.

He pushed me off his lap and stood up, putting the laptop into the bag with the papers. Once everything was away, he took a deep breath and smiled at me. His shoulders dropped down to their proper position, and he looked far calmer. I wondered what could possibly be in that bag that had him so anxious to keep it private.

"You okay?" I asked, trying to get my bearings. I had been expecting warm kisses by now.

"Yes," he said, but his head shook no. "Just catching up on work stuff. Lawyers stress me out. You want to go get some breakfast?"

"I can't," I replied, looking around the room for my clothes. I had thought I had taken them off here, but I didn't see them.

"Room service again?" Logan asked, wrapping me up in his arms. This was the morning greeting I had been expecting. He pulled me in to him, his bare chest against mine. Between his skin and the panty-dropping smile he was using, I was tempted to stay. Very tempted.

"I can't," I said, kissing him softly before disentangling myself from his arms. "While room service does sound wonderful, I need to go check my email."

I saw my shirt peeking out from beneath the couch and pulled it out. Logan was right behind me as I stood, nipping on the soft spot of my neck and sending shivers down my spine. His breath was hot and welcome on my skin. "You sure?"

I let myself relax against him again, his kisses teasing the delicate skin of my neck and the shirt nearly falling from my fingers. "I can't," I managed to say a final time, though not without hesitation. I stepped away and turned to look him in the face. "I have this little business problem I'm trying to fix today."

He grimaced slightly. "Right. That. I promise, I'm doing what I can to make it right."

I knew this wasn't his fault. It was his father's. "I really appreciate it. I do." I put the shirt up over my head, starting the process of getting dressed. "You want to get a table for us downstairs? I'll do my best to get through my emails quickly, but then we can at least still have breakfast."

"I'll take you any way I can get you," he answered, his eyes hovering at the bottom hem of my shirt and darkening. He was wearing only a pair of boxers, and I was strongly considering changing my mind yet again. But my phone chirped indicating another urgent message. *Business before pleasure*, I thought. Always business before pleasure.

"I want you to know how incredibly tempted I am just to stay up here," I said. He grinned and I nearly lost my nerve to leave.

"Hurry, then, and we'll eat quickly and come back." He paused, bending over to pick up my shorts and hand them over. He leaned back and watched me finish dressing. As I put on my shoes, he waggled his eyebrows. "Or maybe we'll go destroy your room next."

"I'd like that. I'll see you in fifteen minutes. Maybe twenty, depending on the emails," I promised, going to the door.

"One more thing," he said, crossing the distance between us and taking me in his arms again. I knew his kiss was coming, but even then, I wasn't prepared for it. He took my breath away, stealing it for himself and making me forget that I had ever needed to breathe in the first place. My knees went weak, and my heart pounded in my chest as my body started to heat. I melted into him, relishing his kiss. This was the way to start a morning.

"That's better than coffee," I gasped when he let me go. He chuckled, obviously proud of himself.

"There's more where that came from," he assured me, sauntering back to his office chair. I took one last look at his broad shoulders, enjoying the view and the pleasant tingling sensation that his visage caused in my nether regions. Today was going to be a very good day.

***

I slid my key card into the door and waited for the green light to flash in recognition. I never trusted these electronic hotel locks. I had accidentally stored one too many of them in the same pocket as my phone so that they were demagnetized.

"Where were you all day yesterday?" Maddy asked, startling me. I nearly missed the green light because I was too busy bumping my head against the ceiling. "And in the same clothes no less?"

"Maddy, you scared me," I told her, putting a hand to my thumping heart. The little jolt of adrenaline raced through me. "What are you doing here?"

"Just walking by." Maddy came right up next to me, peering into my face and then bursting out in a big grin. "I was right. You've been with someone."

"What?" I chuckled nervously. I wasn't ready for this conversation yet. I hadn't had my coffee, and while Logan's kiss was the best way to wake up, I wasn't ready to face the wrath of Momma Maddy without my caffeine. "I have no idea what you're talking about."

Maddy laughed, clearly enjoying my discomfort. "You met a boy. Or rather, judging from that happy glow you're giving off, you met a man."

I nearly slipped putting the key card in a second time, but I at least managed to get the door open. Maddy followed me inside, practically bouncing with excitement.

"Maddy, I have no idea what you're talking about." I tried to keep my face serious, but she knew me far too well. She hugged me and giggled.

"Tell me all about him. I want to know everything." She grinned. She was so happy for me. Both of us had struggled with the dating world the past two years, so I knew she saw either one of us getting any action as a victory for both of us.

I sighed. There was no way I was getting out of this. At least I didn't have to tell her who it was. "Maddy..." I had no idea what to say next. *Maddy, I'm sleeping with my biggest rival and the man who already broke my heart once. And I think I'm falling for him again. Because, I'm just that smart.* Yeah. That would go over really well.

"I haven't seen you this happy in a long time. I was a little worried about you," Maddy confessed. "But right now, you're radiant. Love looks good on you."

"It's not love," I said a little too quickly, feeling a blush settle in my cheeks.

Maddy raised her eyebrows. "If you say so. Whatever it is, at least the sex makes you look good."

"Maddy!" My blush went deeper.

"Messy hair, rosy cheeks, a little wiggle in your walk…" Maddy demonstrated, moving her hips in a swivel that made her look like she was going to throw out her back in the process. "It's pretty obvious. Tell me all about him."

I let my arms fall to my side. There was no fighting her. If I just gave her the info she wanted, and left out the Logan part, everyone could go happily to breakfast. If she saw me at breakfast with him, I could say I was being a good businesswoman and considering all my options. That sounded reasonable enough to me.

"Well, he's built like a Greek god and worthy of the legends." I thought of Logan's broad shoulders and the magic his fingers could work. Definitely worthy of the legends. "I was… let's go with hesitant, about him at first. But he's not what I thought. He convinced me to look a little deeper."

"Oh, you've got it bad." Maddy snickered and sat down on the bed, bouncing up and down a little like a middle school sleepover guest. "What's his name?"

"Um…" I turned away from her, digging into my suitcase, and bit my lip. Maddy knew my history with Logan. She was one of the few people that actually understood all of it, and had witnessed its effects on me. Ever since the wedding, she had become extremely protective of me when it came to Logan. I was pretty sure she felt guilty about blabbing to him.

A knock on the door saved me. "I got it," Maddy said, hopping up from the bed. I let out a sigh of relief. Hopefully, it was just housekeeping.

"Hi, Maddy," Logan's voice said from the doorway. "I was just seeing if Olivia was ready for breakfast."

My heart dropped, landed on the floor, and flopped around like a fish. It just *had* to be Logan at the door. I was pretty sure Fate hated me. I held onto a sliver of hope that I could convince her this would be just a business meeting, but I could feel it in my bones that she was going to figure it out. Maddy was a mom. She always figured this stuff out.

"She's getting dressed. How about I have her meet you down at the restaurant?" Maddy was nothing but polite, and I knew that meant trouble. She was never courteous unless it was to a customer or someone she was contemplating killing later. She said the politeness was part of her plan to get away with murder some day. All the witnesses would say it just couldn't have been Maddy because she was always so gracious. Logan was a dead man.

"That sounds wonderful. Would you and Tyler like to join us?" Logan asked. I wanted to kiss him and smack him at the same time. Bless him for trying to find a way to be a part of my life, but this was just digging my grave a little deeper.

"We already ate, thank you," Maddy responded.

"All right. Say hi to Tyler for me," Logan said with a smile in his voice. "I should go get a table before all the good ones are taken. It was nice to see you,

Maddy."

"Thank you, Logan. I'll send Olivia down in just a bit. We have some things we need to discuss," she said, all smiles and sunshine. An icy balloon was growing in the pit of my stomach. The regret I had so successfully ignored up until now was filling up all the hollow spaces in my body. I quickly changed my clothes as Maddy quietly closed the door.

"Please tell me this isn't what I'm thinking it is," she said, coming into the bedroom. She was wearing her worried mom look and I could feel my willpower crumbling against it.

"Maddy, let me explain..."

"Oh my gosh, it is..." Maddy leaned against the doorway, her mouth hanging open. Disappointment was written all over her face. "What is there to explain? You're sleeping with the man who not only tried to ruin your business once, but is actively trying to do it again? Not to mention, the last time he slept with you he never bothered to call you back? What are you thinking?"

"He didn't have anything to do with the business!" I interjected. I hated that disapproving look. I would take angry, upset, or horror over disappointed any day of the week.

"Olivia..." Maddy pressed her fingertips into her forehead and took a steadying breath. "Don't you see what he's doing?"

"He didn't have anything to do with the consultants, Maddy. He feels terribly about all of it. He's even trying to help," I told her, desperate to explain. I couldn't handle her stricken gaze.

"He's using you!" she exclaimed, swiftly crossing the space between us and resting her hands atop my shoulders so she could shake them.

"What?" Her words didn't make any sense. I stepped back, but she didn't let go.

She sighed and spoke slowly. "He wants your company. For the past six months, you haven't given it to him. He's tried everything to get it. And it hasn't worked, so he's trying a new tactic."

"No..." I shook my head, but she wouldn't let me go.

"He gets you to like him. Trust him. Believe that he's looking out for your best interests." Maddy paused and pressed her lips together for a moment. "How long do you think you'll be able to keep telling him you're not selling when you're sleeping in bed with him?"

"It's not like that, Maddy," I said, trying to figure out what it actually was like myself. With her words in my ear, I wasn't quite so sure anymore. Doubt was creeping into regret's spot in my stomach.

"Then what is it like? From where I'm standing, a shrewd, conniving businessman is reaching you where you are most vulnerable. As soon as you give him what he wants, he's going to leave you high and dry...again." She frowned, her eyes concerned. What scared me more than anything was that she wasn't even angry.

"He wouldn't..." I repeated breathlessly.

"How can you say that after what he did to you? If it hadn't been for him, you would have had backers like Travel-Pedia and HotelVacations two years ago."

She stopped and took a deep breath. "He led you on for the benefit of Travel, Inc. And now he's doing it again, but you're too charmed by his six-pack abs and empty promises to see it. But this time, it's going to be even worse. I won't be able to save you this time."

Tears welled up in my eyes. What if she was right? What if this was just another one of Logan's amazing business negotiation tactics? I didn't want to be used again. But he had been so honest and sincere yesterday. It had felt real, more real than anything I had ever had with another person.

"He's promised to help me fix this," I said meekly, still unwilling to doubt him in full. "He's sincere about it. I know it."

"And he hasn't given you any reason not to trust that? I mean, even if we negate past experiences with him, he hasn't done anything that makes you think he might be hiding something from you?" Maddy asked. I instantly remembered when he slammed his laptop shut this morning.

"No. He hasn't done anything to make me doubt him." It wasn't really a lie. Maddy didn't need to know what had happened this morning after I startled him. Besides, he had every right to be startled. I would have reacted the same way.

Maddy looked at me, evaluating my words before speaking. "You remember meeting my ex-husband, Tom, right? You shook his hand and he smiled and was incredibly charming?"

I nodded. I had met him only once, but he had seemed very nice.

"And I bet you wondered for a moment, 'Is

Maddy crazy? This is a great guy!'" Maddy paused just long enough for me to start denying it before she cut me off. "But you saw what he did to me. How he was so sweet and kind and caring about the whole affair. He apologized so many times and I believed him."

"I remember," I said softly.

She sniffled and wiped her eye with her hand. "And then he took everything. And because I had trusted him--because I thought his lies were sincere promises--he got it all. He left Tyler and me with nothing because I trusted him when he said he had 'only good intentions' toward me."

I remembered that part, too. I met Maddy just as the divorce proceedings had started. Things had seemed to be amicable on the surface, but the lying, cheating bastard had abused Maddy's innocence and love. He took almost everything in the divorce simply because he could.

"Tell me you don't see the parallel here. Tell me that Logan, and all his tactics and charm, doesn't remind you of Tom." Maddy held onto me, forcing me to look her in the eye instead of down at the floor. The parallels were strong, but surely Logan was a better person than Tom. As much as I loved Maddy, I knew I was better at reading people. But when I met Maddy's pleading gaze, I wasn't so sure about anything anymore.

Maddy was one of the sharpest people I knew. Nothing seemed to get by her, and yet Tom had taken advantage of her, time and again. Could I be missing what Logan was doing in the same way? Was Maddy right? Was love blinding me? I wasn't sure.

"I'm not trying to destroy your happiness. I'm really not. I'm trying to do you a favor here. Don't be me." She let go of my shoulders and sighed. "Just don't believe his sweet words and leave your business unguarded."

I looked down at my hands. I was so confused. Logan and Maddy each pulled on my heartstrings and unsettled my mind. How on earth was I supposed to chose?

"Even if he is exactly what he says he is, even if the evil Travel, Inc. company did all of this without his knowledge, is Logan Hayes of Travel, Inc. someone that Olivia Statler of Dream Vacations should be associating with?" Maddy asked, switching to a more logical tactic.

When I didn't respond, she continued, "If he can't buy your company, he's going to become your biggest competition. His company, with or without his consent, stole our top consultants. If Travel, Inc. can't get ownership of Dream Vacations, they are going to make their own. With that in mind, where do you see this relationship going?"

I didn't have an immediate answer for that. I had been so caught up in the moment, in our passionate hurricane kisses, that I hadn't thought of the future. I turned and walked to the window, trying to think. The wind rattled the boards, but we were still safe from the storm outside. I realized I was now accustomed to the roar of the rain and barely even heard it anymore. It was funny how quickly that had happened.

I tried to imagine a future where I still had

complete control over Dream Vacations and also still had Logan. My imagination was not kind. In every scenario I could think of, hostilities were bound to brew up between us like storms. I thought of us trying to talk over dinner about work; thought of meeting his brother; thought of meeting his father.

That last one made me shudder. If his father was willing to go to the work of stealing my consultants away in order to bring down my business, what would he be willing to do if he found out we were together? Not only would both of our lives revolve around our work; we'd be working toward completely opposite goals. Despite my feelings for Logan, I couldn't see a way of us working beyond these hotel walls.

"What do I do, Maddy?" I felt a tear run down my cheek. I turned from the window to face her. "I like him, and I know he likes me. A lot. How do I go downstairs and say, 'Hey, thanks for the fantastic sex and deep conversations, but for business reasons, we're going to have to stop seeing each other.'"

"You say just that. Maybe a little more nicely," she offered with a smile.

"I don't want to hurt him," I whispered. Even though he had once hurt me, I didn't want to turn around and do the same. Once, not that long ago, I would have relished this opportunity. But now ... now, I hated it. I slid to the floor and leaned against the wall. I could feel the strength of the storm outside as it pummeled the siding.

"You have a choice to make, then," Maddy stated logically. "Logan Hayes, billionaire playboy representing your biggest competition, or the business you built with your own blood, sweat, and tears. The business that feeds not only my son and me, but six other women's families? The company of your dreams. It's either Logan, or Dream Vacations, Liv."

I glanced up at her, my eyes welling with fresh tears. I knew she was right. I was responsible for the financial well-being of my employees. That didn't mean I had to like it, though. "Why can't I have both?"

Maddy crossed the room and dropped to her knees to hug me. I felt safe in her arms--not as safe as I did in Logan's, but I knew she loved me and would always do so. "Because life sucks. I'm pretty sure the whole goal of existence is to make things as complicated and difficult as possible."

I let out a shuddering sigh. I wished I had never gotten out of bed. This isn't what I wanted. Not even close, but I knew what I needed to do. Maddy rose and helped me stand.

"You ready?" she asked, once I was up. I stared at the door, desperately racking my brain for an alternative solution. I couldn't find one.

"I hate being an adult," I whined, sounding more like a kid instead. "I don't want to do this."

"Do you want me to do it for you?" Maddy offered. "I'll go down there and do it myself if it will make it easier for you."

"Thank you, but no." I shook my head and took a deep breath. "It needs to come from me. Otherwise, it's too close to what he did to me. I had the hardest time accepting that and letting it go. If I do it, it will be real. If you do it, then there's a chance. I don't want to tempt him with false hope. If he had been the one to call and tell me that Travel, Inc. didn't want me--that our drinks had been fun, but there was nothing for us--I would have believed it and it wouldn't have weighed so heavy on my heart."

Maddy hugged me again. I tried to absorb some of her resolve, but I didn't feel any tougher. She squeezed me tighter. "You can do it. Do you want me to come down with you?"

"Yes," I said timidly. "But stay out of sight. I need to be the one doing this. I can't have you standing there coaching me."

"I'll stay hidden, don't worry," she assured me. "This will all work out in the end."

I nodded absently, opening the door to the hallway. "By the way, where's Tyler?" I asked. I knew it was a distraction, but I needed something better to put in my mind than the fact that I was off to break someone's heart.

"Sleeping in. He spent most of the night with Spock. The room that they have him in echoes really loudly with the wind. Plus, if Tyler isn't with him, the dog gets anxious," she explained.

"I guess they both need each other," I reasoned.

"Yeah, they do." Maddy waited patiently for me to step into the hallway, but I just stood there listening to her tell me about Tyler. "Anyway, I went down and found them both fast asleep in a corner, so I brought Tyler back to sleep in a bed. Poor kid needed some actual rest. Spock should be fine until Tyler wakes up."

I nodded but made no move to leave the doorway.

Maddy gave me a gentle nudge. "Now, stop stalling. Rip off the Band-Aid, or it's just going to hurt worse," she advised me.

I finally moved forward, and Maddy closed the door firmly behind me.

CHAPTER TWENTY-THREE

Logan sat at a table waiting for me. His long legs were crossed off to the side as he flipped through an old newspaper and sipped on a coffee. He looked content and alluring with the candlelight flickering across his handsome face. The lighting in the restaurant was romantic, which felt strange for breakfast, but but since all the windows were boarded over, having candles on each table made sense in case of power outage. I swallowed hard and looked back at Maddy, who was waiting by the elevators. She nodded. I took a deep breath, trying to stop time. It didn't work. I still had to do this.

I paused, taking in the strength of his jaw and the curve of his cheek. That lone curl had fallen across his forehead again. I tried to imagine this scene with the two of us in Chicago. Could we make it work? Was Maddy wrong?

Every last minute scenario I could come up with was terrible. Our businesses always came between us. I wished that his father hadn't turned me down two years ago. If I had joined Travel, Inc. then, I wouldn't be going through this now. Granted, I would have never found out how strong I could be and how much I loved running my own business, but the loss still made my heart ache.

I had to do this. I had to end it my relationship with Logan here, before it had a chance to move off the island and destroy us both. I could almost convince myself that if I stopped us now, it wouldn't hurt. That the connection we had was purely physical. That I wasn't starting to feel things toward him. That I hadn't actually been feeling those things towards him for a long time. Love and hate were such opposite sides of the spectrum, but yet I knew emotions were more like a circle than a line. The distinction between the two was blurry, and I was terribly afraid I had crossed it a long time ago.

Still, this relationship endangered my livelihood. I put everything I had, emotionally and financially, into building and running Dream Vacations. Sleeping with the competition put all that I had worked for in jeopardy. I loved the freedom of owning my own business and making my own decisions. I couldn't give that up. Not for something I wasn't sure was going to last a week outside of the tropical air.

Business was what had kept us apart the last time, too. This romance was doomed from the start. Maddy was right. It was Logan or my company. And right now, my company had the better track record. Logan had the better body, but Dream Vacations was my future.

I squared my shoulders and pulled up the memory of the secretary telling me that Mr. Hayes was no longer interested. I let that hurt wash over me and give me the strength to do this. I could be gentle, but my resolve had to be firm. I walked into the room and sat down across from the man whose heart I was about to break.

His face blossomed into a smile as I sat. He glanced

down at the table, indicating the cup of coffee he'd gotten for me. I could smell the delicious aroma of a vanilla latte. My favorite. My nerve wavered, and I nearly called my plan off. *Be strong*, I told myself. *You can do this. You have to do this.*

"I read in an interview that vanilla lattes were your favorite," Logan admitted. He grinned like a child eager to hear that his surprise was well liked.

"Yes, they are," I said softly, staring down at the light brown liquid. His eyes held that color sometimes. I felt tears forming deep within me. I hated this part. This moment of innocence and calm before the storm was terrible.

"Are you okay?" Logan asked. His enthusiasm had switched to concern. He reached out a hand and placed it on mine.

I pulled my hand away. "No. I'm not." My voice shook as I looked up from the coffee and in to his troubled face. "I'm very sorry, but we can't do this."

"They have a couple of other flavors of lattes," Logan replied, deliberately misunderstanding me. "You can have anything you want."

"It's not the latte," I said quietly. My heart was made of glass and it was shattering. "It's us."

And then I proceeded to break both our hearts.

CHAPTER TWENTY-FOUR

"The hurricane currently pounding on the shores of Antigua and the surrounding islands has been upgraded to a Category 2 hurricane with wind speeds approaching a hundred and ten miles per hour. The storm is dissipating as it moves further South, but conditions are still considered to be dangerous. Residents are advised to stay indoors in a safe location. Power outages and flooding are expected in many areas..."

I stared at the TV screen, not really hearing the reporter's words or even seeing the map. The room was dark except for the glowing screen, and I was simply focused on the light. I wasn't sure how long I had been sitting here, staring at nothing and hating myself, but enough time had passed that the gray light was gone from the windows.

I kept seeing Logan's crumple, seeing the ache and betrayal in his eyes, seeing his broad shoulders slumping as he broke. All I could hear were the tightness in his voice and the loss and pain that echoed through in the pauses between his words. I had hurt him. I had given him hope that we could be happy, and then stripped it all away from him. Having hurt him was what killed me most.

I reached for another Kleenex, but the box was empty. I didn't have the energy to move to find another one or to even get a roll of toilet paper from the bathroom. I just wanted to curl up in a tiny ball and let the storm swallow me whole. It was what I deserved.

Worst. Vacation. Ever.

A frantic banging on my door finally roused me from my stupor. I staggered to my feet and opened it to see a very pale Maddy.

"Have you seen Tyler?" she asked, peeking around me to see if he was in my room. Her hair was a mess and her voice wrought with anxiety. A jolt of fear woke me up from my own problems.

"No, I haven't," I told her, opening the door wider to let her in. "Is everything okay? What's going on?"

She paced the living room nervously, the clunk of her walking boot only adding to my anxiety. Her hands twisted a bracelet around her wrist in a quick motion. She only did that when she was extremely distressed. "I took a nap this afternoon, and when I woke up, Tyler wasn't in the room. I went down to check on him and Spock, but neither one of them was there."

"I'm sure they're around here somewhere, Maddy," I consoled her. "They must have just gone for a walk or something."

"None of the staff has seen them." She stopped mid-pace and looked up at me with eyes as wide as saucers. "Keiko said she saw the door to Spock's area open earlier."

"They can't have gone far. Tyler knows not to go out in the storm," I told her, but I was already putting on my shoes to go look for him.

"But Spock doesn't," Maddy countered, worry dripping off of every syllable. "That dog hated being in that room and with the door open... I'm scared Tyler went after him. What if they found a way out into the storm?"

I stood from putting my shoes on and put my hands on her shoulders. She was shaking. "It's going to be okay. We'll find him. I promise. They're probably just in one of the kitchens stealing cookies or something."

She followed me out into the hallway and down to the main lobby. Dr. James was talking to the concierge, Keiko. Both their expressions were troubled.

"Ms. Sawyer," Keiko addressed her as she saw us approach. "Have you found him yet?"

Maddy shook her head. She was struggling to hold it together. Dr. James and Keiko glanced at one another. Dr. James pressed his lips into a thin line that communicated all too well what he was thinking.

Keiko picked up the phone. "Security?" she clarified in her calming voice. "Yes. We have a missing boy. Eleven years old. Light brown hair, brown eyes. Thin build. Last seen wearing...?" she asked, looking at Maddy.

"A blue t-shirt and gray cargo shorts," Maddy supplied quickly. Keiko nodded and repeated Maddy's words into the phone.

"Can either of you think of where he might have gone?" Dr. James asked, drawing our attention to him. "Has he made any friends his own age here? Could he be in someone else's room?"

"No," Maddy said, shaking her head. "The only friend he has is that dog. He'll be wherever the dog is."

I put my hand on Maddy's shoulder as she leaned against the desk. A shriek of wind rattled the boards holding the storm at bay. I swallowed hard and prayed that security found him quickly.

"What's going on?" Logan asked, walking up to the

concierge desk. I hadn't even heard him approach. He looked remarkably put together. I was sure I looked like a mess. I hadn't even bothered to brush my hair before coming down. He refused to look at me, focusing instead on Dr. James.

"Ms, Sawyer's son is missing," Dr. James supplied. "You haven't happened to see an eleven-year-old boy running around, by any chance?"

"Tyler's missing?" Logan froze. "Where's Spock?"

"Maddy can't find him or the dog anywhere," I answered. Logan didn't look at me, but he paled.

Keiko set down the phone. She glanced at the faces around the desk before delivering her news. "Security just did a sweep of the bathrooms, kitchens, and maintenance hallways and didn't find him. One of the guards remembers seeing a dog running through the maintenance hallway a little after lunch, though. He says strays get in there occasionally and didn't think much of it until now. They're going to start checking the rest of the buildings."

"Could they be lost in the maintenance hallway?" Maddy asked, fear and hope thrumming in her voice. Lost was bad, but at least they were safe from the storm.

"No. Security checked them all." Keiko hesitated, her eyes going to Dr. James before continuing. "But that hallway leads to the other buildings. Ones that aren't as secure against the storm. If they went in there, they could have gotten outside."

Everyone fell silent for a moment. The wind howled and shook the doors. The lights flickered slightly as the storm demonstrated its power.

"We have to find them," I whispered, more to myself than to anyone else. I looked at the boarded-up doors, starting to think of ways to search out in the storm.

"You said the dog is missing too?" Logan asked quietly. His eyes were on me now for the first time since his arrival, watching me contemplate the entrance. I could practically see the gears in his brain turning.

"He wasn't in the room that we were keeping him in," Maddy answered. She was twisting her bracelet at a rate I was sure was going to give her friction burns. "He must have escaped."

"I have an idea where they might be. "Logan stood taller. "Somewhere the dog would go to feel safe. Where's that maintenance hallway?"

Keiko pointed to the doorway behind and to her left. "He was in storage room three. There's diagrams at each junction."

Logan moved quickly toward the door and I caught his arm. He froze at my touch, his muscles tense and hard. "Where are you going?" I asked.

He gently extracted his arm from my grip but didn't look at me. "When we first met Spock, he was sleeping in the shed with the jet-ski equipment. I'm guessing that's where Spock went and where Tyler followed him."

"The hallway doesn't extend that far. You'd have to go out in the storm," Dr. James informed us. He looked to Maddy. "Would Tyler have done that?"

Maddy thought for a moment and her face crumpled. "Yes. He loves that dog. He would have followed him through fire."

"It's amazing the things you'll do for the ones you love," Logan said quietly. He glanced at me for a moment before shifting his gaze. A lump formed in my throat that threatened to strangle me.

"I'm going to that shed," Maddy announced.

"No," Logan said firmly. "If I'm wrong, and he's still in the building, you need to be here. Besides, you have a cast. I'll go."

"I'm going with you," Dr. James informed him. "You don't know where you're going, but I do. There's raincoats in the service entrance."

Keiko opened the door for Logan and handed Dr. James a flashlight and walkie talkie from beneath the desk. I followed behind them, glancing back at Maddy before disappearing into the hallway. She nodded at me. She wanted someone to go with them who knew Tyler.

The sound of rain and wind echoed into infinity against the concrete walls as we hurried inside. Neither man said anything to me as we pushed down the corridor. Dr. James led with his flashlight ready in case the power went out. In these enclosed hallways, it would be pitch black the second the lights failed.

We passed the room where Spock had been staying. The light was still on inside, illuminating the fact that the boy and his dog were missing. I swallowed hard, fighting to stay calm against the panic growing in my chest. Tyler had to be okay. He had to be.

We walked quickly and silently. The howl of the storm filled our ears like constant thunder the closer we got to the exit. Finally we came to a heavy door at the end of the hallway. Dr. James went to a panel and pulled out three raincoats. Mine was too big, but I put the yellow plastic jacket on anyway.

"This is as close as we can get to the storage shed," he told us and then checked in with his walkie talkie. I could hear Keiko on the other end. Dr. James looked at the two of us and then turned and opened the door.

The sky was molten lead. Rain was pouring down and bouncing off the already saturated ground and then hurrying back to the sea to do it again. The trees on either side of the door struggled against the wind as their roots barely held them in place. Leaves, rocks, and pieces of wood littered the ground in haphazard piles that fluttered in the wind and then flew into the air. Every fiber of my being told me not to go out in this storm. The fury of the storm terrified me. The last time I had been out in the storm, it had been a delicate spring shower compared to this.

The walkie talkie squawked just as Dr. James was about to step out. He held it to his ear and then cursed. "Shit. There's been an accident. Window broke and someone's been cut. I have to go back."

"Go," Logan told him. "I know the way."

Dr. James evaluated him for a moment and then nodded solemnly. He pressed the speak button on the walkie talkie and held it to his mouth. "On my way. Giving the walkie to our searchers." He handed me the heavy plastic device and flashlight. "Good luck, you two."

I watched him speed back down the flickering hallway. We were alone now. I didn't dare look at Logan. As Dr. James disappeared around a corner, a little more fear crept into my heart.

Logan didn't hesitate. The moment Dr. James was gone from sight, Logan struck out to find Tyler. He squared his broad shoulders against the wind and tucked his head, moving forward with purpose toward the storage shed. Luckily it wasn't far. I took a deep breath, stuffed the walkie and flashlight into my pocket, and stepped out into the storm to follow him.

The strength of the wind took my breath away. It was as if the air were moving too fast and was filled with too much water for me to be able to breathe. The rain pelted my raincoat with tiny, angry hammers. A gust of wind caught me, and I felt my feet slide out from under me. I wondered for a moment if I would simply fly away like a kite, but instead I fell into a puddle with a thud.

Logan reached down and picked me up. "Hold onto me," he shouted. I clung to his waist, using his weight and size to stay anchored against the wind. He pushed relentlessly on toward the shack.

The wind whipped at my too-big raincoat, alternating between turning it into a second skin and trying to tear it from my body. I was tiny and powerless against this storm. Without Logan to protect me, I felt like I was going to be ripped up into the air at any moment.

He stopped and pointed to the shed. It was still there, but it didn't look like it was going to stay that way for long. Most of the roof was missing with the broken pieces scattered around the ground. My heart was pounding in my throat. I prayed that Tyler wasn't in there. I needed him to be safe and sound somewhere far from the rain and wind.

Together we crept forward, finally coming to the door. Logan pushed it open, and I shined the flashlight inside.

"Tyler?" Logan boomed, but his voice only lasted a second before the wind stole it. "Tyler!"

A small movement caught the edge of the light. "Tyler!" I screamed, launching myself forward to get to him. Logan stopped me in my tracks with his arm and shook his head.

"It isn't stable," he shouted into the wind. I looked at him and realized I could hear the building creaking and groaning. I peered into the shed, moving the flashlight back and forth, desperate to save Tyler somehow.

Debris was scattered randomly among upturned jet-skis and miscellaneous water-sport equipment. My flashlight bounced off two glowing eyes. Spock woofed gently, his tail wagging in greeting as he recognized us.

"Come here, boy," I called, kneeling down and patting my leg. Spock took a single step forward before sitting down next to an upturned jet-ski and pile of plywood. I gasped as I recognized Tyler's shoe poking out from under the wreckage.

Logan saw it, too. "Wait here and give me light," he commanded. I barely heard him over the wind, but I nodded and focused the yellow beam of light on Tyler's shoe. Logan stepped gingerly over the threshold, glancing nervously at the creaking building.

My heart was simultaneously in my throat and stomach. I wanted to follow him, to do something helpful, but I knew providing the light and not getting in the way was the best thing I could do. I bit my lip, nearly drawing blood.

Logan lifted a broken piece of wood from on top of Tyler and hurled it to the side. A toppled jet-ski had pinned Tyler's leg to the ground. Logan raised it, struggling with its awkward weight for a moment before righting it. He picked up Tyler's small form and cradled him to his chest. Tyler's hand dangled limply to the side.

"Tyler..." I whispered to the wind. A sob caught in my throat. He was so small and fragile in Logan's arms. The limp hand moved and balled into the coat at Logan's chest. My heart decided to beat again as Logan exited the shed, Spock right at his heels.

I led the way this time. Holding onto the makeshift bandana collar Tyler had given Spock and the flashlight, I took us back down the beach to the heavy hallway door. Spock pressed into my leg, as if he knew that if I let go he would fly away. Logan held onto me while he shielded Tyler with his body as sand and water peppered our backs. At least it was easier going this way.

I pushed open the heavy door to the maintenance hallway for Logan and Spock to enter. Stumbling in behind them, I looked down the beach toward the shack as I pulled the door shut. The storage shed was gone. A low, sick feeling filled the pit of my stomach. If Logan hadn't thought of where they might be...

I slammed the door shut against the storm. The rain and wind stopped pelting us, but the sounds of both filled the hallway. Tyler was pressed into Logan's chest, but he was breathing and awake. I pulled the walkie talkie from my pocket. "This is Olivia. We've got him. He's injured, but we've got him."

"Roger that, Olivia." Dr. James' voice crackled over the connection. I could hear Maddy crying in the background. "I'm in the lobby. Bring him home."

"Spock?" Tyler's feeble voice asked, his head lifting to search for his beloved dog.

"He's here. We got him, too," Logan told him. "We got you both. You're safe now."

Tyler relaxed his head onto Logan's shoulder, but he kept his death grip on Logan's raincoat. Logan's eyes met mine for a brief moment. Their depths reflected the simultaneous relief and urgency I knew were in mine. Without another word, Logan turned and moved quickly back down the hallway toward the main lobby. Spock was right behind them, eyes up on Tyler's feet. One of his ankles didn't hang correctly and was already swelling. I swallowed down the lump in my throat as I scrambled after them, hoping that the obviously broken ankle was the worst of Tyler's injuries.

The storm howled against the tunnel and the lights flickered, but we didn't stop. Logan followed the path as if he had walked it a thousand times and before I knew it, we were to the lobby. Spock whined softly at Logan's heels, frustrated that he couldn't touch his master. I petted his head, unsure if the gesture was meant to soothe the dog or me, but it had a calming effect on both of us as we hastened after the man and boy.

Keiko was waiting for us and holding the door open. Warm yellow light from the lobby spilled onto the gray cement floor, beckoning us onward. Logan's pace increased, and I hurried my own to keep up. Safety lay in the direction of the lobby.

Maddy cried out Tyler's name as Logan emerged from

the doorway and into the light of the lobby. She was at Tyler's side in a heartbeat, brushing the hair from his forehead and kissing his cheeks. Tears of relief ran down Maddy's face as she took in her son and thanked Logan profusely in a language that had been English before her emotion choked her words.

"Set him down here so I can check him out," Dr. James instructed Logan, pointing to a chaise lounge in the lobby. Logan gently set the boy down on the green cushioned chair, careful to protect his ankle. Tyler clung to Logan's raincoat for a moment before finally letting his rescuer go. Spock lay obediently down on the floor at Tyler's feet, his eyes fixed firmly on his master.

Dr. James dropped his medical bag to the ground and quickly started checking Tyler out, moving efficiently and smoothly as he made sure the ankle was the worst of Tyler's problems. Tyler's brown hair was plastered to his head from the rain, contrasting with the paleness of his skin. Maddy stroked his head, gazing at her baby boy, her eyes brimming with tears of love.

Logan backed away slowly from the chaise lounge, and was slowly drifting from the group. I could tell he was trying to escape before anyone noticed. I blocked his path.

"You didn't have to do that," I said, crossing my arms.

"Do what?" he asked, innocence painted on every word.

"Go out in a hurricane for a kid you barely know." I searched his face trying to figure out why he had risked his life for Tyler. I was willing to go out there because I loved Tyler like he was my own and Dr. James was willing because it was his job to help people. But Logan? He was a billionaire playboy who, without me, had no connection to Tyler. Since our connection was no longer intact, he had no obligation to do anything.

Logan's dark eyes searched my face for a moment.

"Then you don't know me very well." He stepped to the side and walked around me, heading toward the elevators. I wanted to chase him down and hold him close, thank him for saving Tyler, and tell him how much I cared for him. But I couldn't. Not after this morning. Instead, I watched him walk away, feeling the hole in my heart growing larger with his every step.

I looked back at Tyler. He was smiling at something the doctor had said. His mother was holding onto him, tears running down her cheeks. I stood and let myself feel relief and gratitude that Tyler was safe. When Tyler's eyes found mine, I went to him.

"It looks like it's just a broken ankle, but we'll still need x-rays. That pain medication should last a few hours," Dr. James said as I approached. "He's still in shock, so we'll need to keep an eye on him, but he should be fine. Let's get him dried off, warmed up, and rehydrated. I'll go get something to immobilize this."

Dr. James ruffled Tyler's hair and stepped away. I went to my knees in front of the couch, putting myself at Tyler's eye level. I thanked the heavens that he had more color in his cheeks and was sitting up by himself. I had been terrified that he had been injured far worse than just a broken ankle.

"Hi, Aunt Liv," he greeted me. I could see the stress of pain around his eyes, but he smiled anyway. Maddy had his hand firmly in hers. It looked as though she wasn't going to let go of it until he was in his thirties.

"You gave us a pretty good scare," I said, putting my hand on his shoulder. Touching him made everything suddenly very real. Something inside me broke, and a tear trickled down my face. I quickly wiped it away.

"I'm really sorry about that." He looked up at his mother and gave us both an apologetic smile. "I had to find Spock, though."

"Next time, let someone know where you're going," Maddy said gently. Her face fluctuated between being anger and relief. "I can't believe you just went off into the storm like that."

"I didn't mean to!" Tyler explained, sitting up further. Maddy pressed his shoulders back down and he didn't fight her. "I thought he might be in that hallway and then I found an open door and I realized that Spock was probably at the shack. I didn't think it was going to be that windy. I got to the shack and tried to drag him out, but he was scared. And then the wind picked up again and that jet-ski flipped." He paused, and he looked down at his knees. "I'm sorry, Mom."

"I'm just so glad you're okay." Maddy kissed his forehead. "You scared me."

Tyler took the hand that wasn't trapped in his mother's grip and reached for the floor. Spock wiggled up to try and reach him, and almost all the way into my lap in the process. His pink tongue kissed Tyler's fingers and his tail thumped against the floor.

"Mom, can we keep Spock? I don't want to leave him here." Tyler's voice cracked.

"Considering you went out in a hurricane to find him, we have to," Maddy conceded. "I'd hate to see what you'd do if I left him here."

I laughed softly. Tyler would be on a plane out here so fast he'd be here before his mom even knew the credit card was missing.

"How did you find me?" Tyler asked, his eyes looking up at me from Spock. "I thought we were goners."

"Logan figured it out," I told him. "He remembered seeing Spock at that storage shed when we went jet-skiing."

Tyler nodded slowly, his eyes glancing around the room for Logan. His smile dimmed a little when he realized that his hero wasn't there. "Thank you for coming to get me, Aunt Liv. You and Logan." He paled slightly. "I was really scared."

I rose up higher on my knees and kissed his forehead. "Me, too," I whispered before settling back into my original spot.

Tyler petted Spock's head. His mother started doing the same thing to him and the parallel of love and care made me smile. Tyler thought for a moment and then looked up at me with serious, big brown eyes. "Aunt Liv?"

"Yeah?" I answered with a soft smile.

"Will you find Logan for me?" he asked. "I didn't get to thank him."

"I'll do my best," I promised.

"And Aunt Liv?" Tyler caught me in his eyes. The pain medication was kicking in and he struggled to focus on me, but he looked serious. "Logan loves you. He can't tell you that, but he does. I was supposed to keep it a secret, but I thought you should know."

I opened my mouth, but nothing came out. Maddy judiciously avoided my gaze. "What?"

"I asked him why you hated him. He said it was because he hurt you." Tyler frowned. "I think you should forgive him. He's a good person."

"It's not quite that simple, Tyler..." I rubbed my forehead, trying to figure out what I could say to make him understand.

"Yes, it is," Tyler contradicted me. "Love is always simple. It's just our brains that make it complicated." He smiled down at Spock. "If you love someone, you find ways to stay with them. Spock taught me that."

I didn't have a good response for that. I could see Dr. James headed our direction with Keiko right behind him carrying blankets and towels, so I stood to give them space to work. Dr. James took my place as I stepped back.

Tyler looked up at me, silently asking for me to get Logan while they worked on him. I sighed and nodded, turning to go look for him. The things we would do for the people we loved...

CHAPTER TWENTY-FIVE

I finally found Logan in the spa lobby. When the resort officially opened, this lobby would be busy with vacationers coming to get massages and pedicures, but with just us few travel agents and a hurricane in full force, the lobby was empty and quiet. It was the perfect place to be alone.

Logan was looking at a picture hanging on the main wall, his hands resting behind is back. The ocean, calm and gentle, filled the frame. Blues and greens that exemplified a tranquil, tropical, and relaxing vacation getaway stood in stark contrast with the howls and shrieks of the wind outside.

I knew he could hear my footsteps on the bamboo flooring, but he didn't move. I stood beside him, examining the picture. The only indication that he knew I was there was the slight stiffening of his body. He didn't move to leave, though.

"Tyler sent me to find you," I finally said, breaking the

silence between us. "He didn't get to say thank you."

"He doesn't need to," he replied.

"He doesn't see it that way," I informed him. I looked at him, taking in his profile. Logan's hair was still damp from the rain, but that curl was back on his forehead. "He said something else that I wanted to ask you about."

Logan's jaw tightened, but he didn't move.

"He said you loved me," I told him quietly. He stood still as stone, staring at the picture. "Is it true?"

The only movement in the room was Logan's Adam's apple as he swallowed. His eyes slowly closed as the word came out. "Yes."

I wasn't sure what I was expecting, but that one syllable hit me like a punch. He loved me. Logan Hayes loved me.

"What? Why?" I gasped, reeling from his confirmation. A surge of happiness filled me, followed by a wash of confusion and then despair. He loved me, but we couldn't be together. Star-crossed lovers we were indeed.

He turned from the painting to face me. His eyes were soft and sad. He knew the regret we both felt. The tragedy that was our love. "I fell in love with you the moment you walked in my office," he said simply. "You were so nervous and absolutely adorable. As we talked, I found out you were smart and funny. And driven. Very driven. I couldn't help it. That's why I asked you for drinks."

I nodded, remembering that night; the giddy happiness I felt at being asked out on a date. The way his eyes had shone during our deeply intense discussions; the simple joy I had felt at seeing him smile and even the happiness at waking up the next morning and thinking I would see him again. As improbable as love at first sight was, I had fallen in love with him then, too.

A soft smile flitted across his face as he remembered as well. "Then you showed up for drinks looking sexy as hell, and I knew I was yours." He shook his head slowly. "I thought not seeing you would make all those feelings go away. I thought it had to be just infatuation or lust. Love at first sight is something for fairy tales. Things that can have happy endings. Love at first sight doesn't last in real life."

I looked down at my feet. I wanted love at first sight to be real. I wanted this to be my fairy tale, but my shoes were covered in mud and leaves. I was no Cinderella.

"When I came back from Malaysia, I was sure you had forgotten me, that you had moved on and that all those feelings were only on my end. And then I saw you at that wedding," he said softly. I looked up to see a sad smile traipse his face. "And then Maddy..."

"Maddy blabbed that I wasn't over you; that I had those same feelings," I supplied. A ghost of a grin tugged at my lips at the memory. "I was ready to strangle her for that. I'm glad I didn't."

"It put sunshine back in my world," he confessed, looking back at the painting. "I thought... I thought I had a second chance. But you were mad, and you had every right to be. I thought maybe, with enough time, you'd see that I cared. I started looking for excuses to see you at social events. I always seemed to miss you at them, though."

"That's when I started avoiding you," I said slowly. "I hated that Maddy gave me away and I didn't want to remember that you broke my heart after just one date. So, I hid from you."

He nodded slowly. Regret and lost hope filled his voice. "You don't want to know how many events I went to, hoping that you would be there-- hoping I could get another chance-- only to find you had left moments earlier or suddenly declined."

I could imagine. After the wedding, I came up with a plan never to see Logan Hayes again. In addition to my constant Google searches, news article alerts, and myFace stalking, Twitter and all of its over-sharing socialites suddenly became my lookouts. I had alerts set on my phone for all trending posts about Logan Hayes. I had driven up to so many parties, only to leave without even getting out of the car because someone tweeted that Logan was there.

"When I heard you had accepted the invitation to this resort, I took Noah up on his offer to come see it." He gave a dry chuckle. "I'm pretty sure I have a pissed-off employee whose place I stole."

His weak attempt at humor made me smile. When he glanced over at me, I was flooded with emotions: regret, hope, loss, joy, love, sadness, and so many others that I couldn't even place all vied for a place in my consciousness. I stared at the picture of the peaceful ocean, trying to sort my thoughts so I could identify them. I didn't know what to say, so in a bid for time, I blurted, "Why did you go into the storm for Tyler? You didn't have to."

"Because I knew you needed me to." He stated it like it was a simple fact. Like the sky was usually blue and water was wet. "I could see it on your face. You were ready to head out the front door and start searching. I went out in that storm because I knew you were going to."

"I didn't realize I was that obvious," I admitted. He had read me like a book.

"You love Tyler. And he loves you. I had to make sure you were both safe. Losing him would devastate you. Losing you would devastate him." He paused and glanced at me again, his voice going soft. "And me as well. I went out in the storm to keep that from happening."

We both focused at the painting again. We were silent, but the roar of the storm outside reverberated off the walls of the sap lobby. I needed to sit down and think. Possibly with wine. No, definitely with wine. Possibly with 151 rum. I was done with emotional upheavals for the day.

One thought was clear, though, as it sailed through the storm in my mind. Logan had risked his life to save Tyler, and by extension, me. He loved me. He had always loved me, just as I had always loved him.

But that didn't matter. The original problem-- the one that had kept us apart in the first place-- still existed. We were competitors, and our love was too fragile to survive in the harsh business world. We'd already proven that once. As much as I was tempted to try again, I knew it would be a futile exercise.

So I stayed quiet, and didn't tell him how much I loved him back; how just one glance from him sent my whole day into a giddy daydream; how I had dreamed of him for two years straight.

No, to save ourselves from another tragic ending, I said nothing and just stood there, contemplating a painting and listening to the rain. I wished my life were more like the tranquil ocean waves of the picture.

"I talked to my father today," Logan said after a long silence. I turned and looked at him. He smiled to himself, still focused on the picture. "I think I'm the first person in a long time to call him an idiot."

I felt my eyes widen and my eyebrows reach for the ceiling. "You said that?"

"More than that. I told him he was wrong. That he was wrong two years ago. That he squandered a prime business opportunity because he couldn't see past his own prejudices. I told him if he didn't want me to take proof of his negligence to the board of trustees in not only this matter, but the six others that I have cleaned up for him, I was to handle all future merger and business acquisitions." He stopped and took a breath before adding, "without him."

I could hardly believe the words coming out of Logan's mouth. I stared at him. "You took him out of the process?

In his own company?"

Logan shrugged as if it were nothing. As if he hadn't just defied thirty-two years of seeking his father's approval. "He's been talking about retirement for a while now. I simply put a timeline on it."

"Wow," I whispered. This was far more than just putting his father on track to retire. From what I understood, Gerald Hayes was not a man who liked being resisted. Part of the reason he was so successful was because he was ruthless and incredibly controlling. And now, Logan had threatened to revoke that control. It was Zeus taking down the Titans. "How did your father take it?"

"Not well," he said flatly, shifting his weight slightly. "But I got what I wanted. If I took half of what I have to the board, he would be drawn and quartered right there in the boardroom."

"I didn't know it was that bad." I was back to studying the painting.

"He's made some bad decisions. I just finally realized that I don't have to be the one who suffers for his mistakes. He'll be retiring at the end of the fiscal year, and my brother and I will be taking over the company. He won't be running things anymore," Logan explained.

"Wow." I couldn't believe it. Logan had taken control of his destiny. "That's some big news."

"Yeah," he said, cracking a smile. He ran a hand through his tangled curls. It was a relaxed and natural motion that relieved the tension in his shoulders. He was free of his father for the first time in his life.

I swallowed hard as I wondered about the question brewing in my mind. I decided to ask it. After today, the worst he could do was not to gratify me with an answer. "Did you do it for me?"

There was a long pause. "Yes and no," he responded

carefully. "It needed to be done. You just gave me the impetus to do it. You defied him with your success and showed me that I can't thrive in his shadow anymore."

I looked down at my shoes again and nodded. "I'm happy for you. You're going to do great." I just wished he had done this two years ago. Things would have been so much simpler. It felt too late now.

"Well, actually, as the soon-to-be CEO and department head of mergers and acquisitions, I do have some business I need to attend to." Logan turned away from the painting. He didn't move closer to me, but somehow I felt like the space between us grew smaller. "I'd like to offer you one last proposal. One I've wanted to give you for a long time, but one which my father would never approved of."

My throat was suddenly dry as I watched Logan dig around in his pocket. For a moment, I thought he was going to drop to one knee and propose. What would I say? Yes? I had no idea.

Instead he handed me a neatly folded piece of paper.

"I'd like to offer you a partnership. Dream Vacations and Travel, Inc." He smiled and looked down at the paper in my hands. "You would keep your company exactly the way it is, just with access to Travel, Inc.'s resources."

I unfolded the paper and stared at it. It was a typical-looking contract, but my eyes were blurring with tears and I couldn't read the legalese. This would solve everything.

"I don't want to be competitors anymore," he said softly, taking my shaking hands in his. I looked up and focused on the warm caramel of his eyes. "I want to be partners. If Dream Vacations succeeds, then Travel, Inc. succeeds and vice-versa."

"I'd get to keep my company?" I gasped. "And still be part of yours?"

"Yes." He nodded. A smile was waiting to blossom fully onto his face if I gave the right answer. "You will have to go to board meetings. And I'm expecting several one-on-one meetings between the CEO of Travel, Inc and Dream Vacations. Don't worry, though, I hear he's cute."

I laughed, tears running down my cheeks. "Yes. Yes, I will partner with you!"

His face split into a grin that made my heart soar. In a smooth motion, he tipped his head forward and kissed me. Our teeth clicked together because we were both smiling so broadly that we couldn't stop, but I didn't care. It was a great kiss.

"Promise me I won't lose you again," Logan requested when we pulled back to catch our breath. Hope and happiness filled his face. I felt like I could burst from too much joy.

"This time I have a contract." I held up the paper and grinned. "You're stuck with me now."

He kissed me again before I could even think, dipping me back in a liplock that would make a Hollywood director proud. I giggled as he released me from his kiss, but not from his arms.

"You'll have to get Maddy's approval on this," I told him. "She owns a fair chunk of the company."

Logan shrugged. "I just walked through a hurricane to save her son. I think I've got enough brownie points to pull that off."

This time, I kissed him. I pulled him in to me, tasting his lips and sharing my joy. We could be together. Our love, and our businesses, would flourish more together than they ever would apart. Outside, the sounds of the hurricane raged and screamed, but when I was with Logan, there wasn't a storm we couldn't weather.

ꝏꙭ ꙭꝏ

EPILOGUE

The ocean breeze is soft against my skin. The water is calm this time, and the sky is blue. I would almost call it a perfect day, except that in my mind, the perfect day here involved a hurricane.

But that was a whole year ago.

Today is about celebrating. Celebrating that storm and how it brought Logan and I together.

"You ready?" Maddy asks, adjusting the straps of her sundress one last time.

"I am," I say. I take a deep breath.

"All right, then, let's get this party started." She grins and takes my hand as we step onto the beach. The wind makes the hem of my dress flutter around my ankles. It's nothing fancy, just a white cotton sundress that is comfortable and soft. There is beauty in simplicity. There's no need to impress anyone with designer labels or couture gowns. We are here just for us.

The sun is almost painfully bright, but I don't care. I can see him. He is like a beacon, shining softly, yet almost more brightly, than the sun itself. He's standing next to his brother and a man in a dark suit. His tall frame stands out against the deep blue of the ocean, and his short curls catch the gentle breeze.

He sees me and I am suddenly the most beautiful thing on the planet. His jaw drops just enough, then widens into a smile like he's won the lottery. I smile, because I know have won the lottery of love.

Maddy stands beside me. Tyler is the only person in the guest area. He had wanted to bring Spock, but Maddy and I had both told him no. We managed to convince him that Spock would be far more comfortable lounging on his bed at home than sitting in the sun.

I smile as I take my place across from Logan. The only people present for the ceremony are the people who care the most about us; the people who have been the most supportive of us and the most understanding of our love.

I glance out at Tyler, and he gives me a big thumbs-up. Logan chuckles.

"Dearly beloved, we are gathered here today..." The minister in the dark suit recites the words to the ceremony in a gentle voice. I've heard them enough times for others that I don't listen. I don't need formal words; I already know in my heart what he is saying. I love Logan, and he loves me. We are joining ourselves together in front of our family and friends so that we never have to be apart again.

I look into Logan's eyes. They are deep pools with glowing embers of love and joy illuminating them. Looking into them, I am content and at peace.

"Repeat after me: I, Logan Hayes..."

HURRICANE KISSES

"I, Logan Hayes," Logan repeats in his deep voice. He sounds nervous, but that makes him all the more loveable. I know he's been looking forward to this for a long time and has been practicing because he doesn't want to mess it up. He wants this to be perfect for me.

Except, everything is already is perfect. As long as he promises to love me, I get to promise the same, and we seal the promise with a kiss, this wedding is all I could ever want. I don't need the perfect words or the perfect dress to have the perfect wedding.

"I promise to be true to you in good times and in bad, in sickness and in health. I will love you and honor you all the days of my life." Logan's hand shakes as he slides my ring onto my finger. He grins once it's situated. Then it's my turn.

"Repeat after me: I, Olivia Statler..."

"I, Olivia Statler..." My voice comes out strong. I've wanted to say these words to Logan almost since the moment I met him. He is my happily ever after. With him by my side, I know we will ride off into the sunset and kiss until the curtain draws. We were made for one another. "I promise to be true to you in good times and in bad, in sickness and in health. I will love you and honor you all the days of my life."

I nearly drop the ring in the sand, but manage to hold onto it. Logan chuckles and I see laughter in his eyes. I slide the shiny metal band on to his finger and I know that this is the beginning of something wonderful. There is so much for us to look forward to, so many dreams and adventures for the two of us to experience. I can hardly wait.

"By the power vested in me, I then declare you husband and wife. You may kiss the bride!"

Logan and I gravitate like magnets toward one another's open arms, and our lips meet in a simple act of love. We kiss, *starting our new life together in an act of love. I can't think of a better way to begin.*

Logan's brother Aiden whoops, and Maddy wolf-whistles. Tyler is busy looking everywhere but at the two of us. Someday, he'll kiss a girl like this and not find it quite so intimidating. The thought makes me smile.

"Congratulations," the minister tells us. He shakes everyone's hand, including Tyler's, and then walks back down the beach toward the resort. The five of us stand in a circle, grinning like idiots. Logan has my hand in his.

"Should we go join the party?" Aiden asks, offering his arm to Maddy. She blushes but quickly takes it.

"You three go on ahead," Logan tells them. "We'll be along in just a minute."

"We'll let the DJ know," Maddy says. "That way you two can make a grand entrance."

Maddy, Tyler, and Aiden follow the minister's footprints back toward the resort, leaving Logan and me alone on our little patch of white sand. Logan takes both my hands in his.

"I love you," he says. It's simple and yet perfect. His eyes shine with affection and joy.

"I love you," I whisper back.

He lets go of one hand to guide me into his kiss. I tangle my fingers in his honey curls, feeling the warmth of the sudden nestled in their midst. He tastes like heaven.

There is a party at the resort where more friends and family are waiting. They can continue to wait. For this moment, I am with the love of my life, and we are celebrating what we have. It took us a long time to finally get it right, but now, the world is ours. Our businesses run together. Our hearts run together. Our worlds are now one.

The wind dances around us, gentle and soft. This kiss is so

HURRICANE KISSES

very different than our hurricane kisses, but yet the same. Love has tempered the storm and made it so that things are now bright and sunny. We are kissing in the sunshine, but thankful for our hurricane kisses.

KRISTA LAKES

A Sneak Peek

SANDCASTLE KISSES:
A BILLIONAIRE LOVE STORY

When Isabel Baker agreed to moonlight as a bartender at a private party, she never imagined she'd get anything more than tips. However, on this resort island, nothing was ever that simple.

After tending bar with the deliciously handsome Noah who was flown in for the party, Izzy realized that she was about to break her number one rule: never fall for a tourist. But with his quick wit, charming smile and passion for marine life, Noah was the kind of guy that she couldn't resist. At the end of the night, she barely managed to turn him away from coming home with her.

Noah had only come to the island for one of Jack Saunders' famous parties. Yet once he met Izzy, he couldn't bring himself to leave. After one steamy night together, he knew that he would do almost anything to keep her.

Theirs should have been an easy love story, complete with a happily ever after. Except Noah was also moonlighting as a bartender that night and his true identity threatened Izzy's research. When his billion-dollar company and her marine research project collide, their entire relationship crumbles into the sand. Will they be able to rebuild their beautiful sandcastle together, or will it be washed away by the rising tide, forever just a memory?

SANDCASTLE KISSES

I peered out of my dirty car window at the big mansion and had to consciously raise my jaw back up off my chest. I knew houses like this populated the island, but I hadn't actually been this close to one before now. Perfect white marble columns were flanked by lush tropical greenery, and scenic balconies hung out at regular intervals. The place was huge. Grandiose. Palatial. It belonged in a movie. And according to my roommate, it was actually one of the smaller mansions of the island. Key Island was the home of two extremely exclusive resorts, a smattering of multimillion dollar homes, and some locals to help run it all. The island was known as *the* island for people with more money than they could spend.

I shook my head as I eased my ancient little Corolla away from the circle of expensive cars in the driveway. My boss hadn't told me much about the job, just to show up and tend bar. I didn't even know who was officially even throwing it. He said there was a place for me to park to the side of the house and then to find Rachel.

Lamborghinis, Maseratis, and Jaguars lined the round-about in front of the house, and the worst part was that most of them were dirty. These people used ridiculously expensive cars as their everyday mode of transportation on the island. If using my entire research grant as a way to get to a party wasn't the epitome of wealth, then I wasn't sure what was.

I followed a delivery truck into a little parking lot off to the side of the house. It had an easy slope up to the big doors of a kitchen and was shaded from view of the house by palms and bushes. At least my little car didn't look quite as out of place as I parked it next to a sensible little blue Honda that was only a year or two younger than mine.

I pulled the keys from the ignition and checked my hair and makeup one last time in the rear-view mirror. My strawberry blonde hair was pulled back in a neat ponytail but with cute little tendrils that framed my face. My hair was now mostly blonde after being in the sun and ocean all day, but I thought it suited me.

My eyeliner was perfect and smooth, making my green eyes pop. I hadn't bothered to try and cover up the smattering of freckles across my cheeks, trusting in my old college roommate who said they were cute. She had taught me how to do my makeup in college and had gone on to become a professional makeup artist, so I figured she had to know what she was talking about.

I practiced a flirtatious smile one more time, checking my teeth in the mirror. With the top button of my white shirt just low enough to display cleavage but not appear slutty, I got out of the car. I tugged on my little black vest until it was straight and took a deep breath. Black pants and some sensible shoes completed my bartender outfit. I hoped I looked cute enough to get some good tips.

The tropical air of the Caribbean island was warm and humid against my skin. It was late afternoon, and the sun was just starting its slow descent down the sky toward blue waters. Birds chirped in the trees, and the beat of dance music started and stopped as someone inside the house worked on getting the sound system set. I felt a tingle of excitement run down my spine. This was going to be a good night.

Just inside the double doors of the kitchen, I found a woman directing traffic. She had on an expensive gray suit, and her dark brown hair was pulled up into a neat bun. Small square glasses were perched on the end of her nose as she peered down at a clipboard and tapped a pen against her lips.

"Are you Rachel?" I asked, stepping up to her. Hers was the only name my boss had given me. She smiled warmly and glanced down at her clipboard.

"Yes. You must be Isabel Baker," she greeted me warmly. I nodded and shook her hand. A man with a keg on a dolly nearly ran me over before Rachel pulled me out of his way. "That goes upstairs on the patio!"

"Do I follow the keg, then?" I asked, my gaze trailing after the man with the keg. Rachel shook her head.

"Nope. You go down to the 'Man Cave.'" She rolled her eyes slightly at the reference, but her smile told me she just thought it was a silly name. "The boys requested to have a real bartender down there tonight. That's where the party will be."

"Oh." I felt a bubble of nerves. This place was incredibly fancy. I hoped I was up to their rich standards. I could feel my palms beginning to sweat.

"Don't worry about them. They just want to relive their glory days," Rachel said warmly, referencing what had to be billionaires like they were her little brothers. "Just don't let them get away with too much. Have fun and don't worry about the booze. Just keep filling up their glasses and smiling, and they'll be happy campers."

"Glasses filled. Got it," I replied.

"If they give you any trouble, just let me know." The dark-haired woman smiled at me and handed me a form to sign. "This is a standard non-disclosure agreement. Your boss said you'd be fine with it."

I quickly scrolled through the form. It seemed pretty straight forward. *Don't tell people who you met here or what they said.* I could understand that famous people wouldn't want to be outed on their vacations or have their drunken ramblings posted across the internet. Signing was easy enough. I handed her back the papers.

Rachel tucked my form behind several others. "Besides that, I'll pay you at the end of the night. Any questions?"

"Just where the 'Man Cave' is," I answered. Rachel's smiled broadened.

"Down that hallway, and then you'll see stairs on your left. Follow the sounds of the boys from there, and you'll find the bar. Remember, have fun. Just tell the guy in the Hawaiian shirt that you're the bartender," she said as a smirk passed over her face at mentioning the Hawaiian shirt.

"Okay, thanks!" I said, but she was already back to her clipboard and chasing after a man wearing a catering uniform. I shook my head. She reminded me of my mom chasing after my little brother and his friends at a birthday party.

I followed Rachel's directions, easily found the stairs, and descended down. "Man Cave" was an excellent term for the room. A tattered but comfortable-looking couch sat in front of a TV big enough to fit in a theater. I could see all sorts of game consoles plugged in and neatly arranged in a massive entertainment system. There was a much-loved pinball machine in the corner and cozy chairs were scattered through the room. The bar took up the far wall, all wooden and shiny with various neon signs overhead. I could see another adjacent room where the DJ equipment was set up. Two men, one blonde and one with sandy hair, were the only party guests I could see so far.

When I stepped from the bottom stair, a large man stepped directly into my path, his arms crossed and an unhappy look on his face. I gulped hard and looked up at his piercing blue eyes. He looked like a sword: thin, limber, and deadly as hell. Then I noticed the brightly patterned shirt with red parrots and blue drinks. It didn't look right on him. It was like a tiger wearing a tutu.

"Um, I'm the bartender," I squeaked. Somehow the

man grew taller. Scarier. He was the big bad wolf from the fairytales and he was going to eat me alive. "The woman upstairs told me to tell the guy wearing the Hawaiian shirt..." my voice faltered.

"Quit scaring the poor girl," someone from the party said, putting a hand on Hawaiian-shirt's shoulder. Hawaiian-shirt winked at me, allowing a hint of a smile peek through his tough facade. I nearly giggled with relief.

"Don't mind Dean. He's just mad that we made him dress up for the occasion," my savior said. "I'm Jack. The bar's this way."

"Izzy," I replied. "Nice to meet you."

I slipped behind the bar and promptly ran into a solid mass of man muscle. I watched in horror as our collision spilled the glass of ice in his hand down the front of his shirt.

"Oh crap! I'm so sorry," I apologized, reaching for some napkins. I found a dry bar towel and held it out to him. He dabbed at his black t-shirt and laughed.

"Don't worry about it. At least it was just ice," he said and handed me back the towel. "I'm Noah. I'm going to be helping you out tonight."

He held out his hand to shake mine. It was warm and strong. My eyes traced from his hand, up perfectly sculpted biceps to a strong jaw and dark hair. His eyes were what made me lose my train of thought, though. They were robin's egg blue and held depths that made my knees weak. Words left my brain. He was flipping gorgeous.

He picked up a new glass and put fresh ice in it to finish making his drink. Vodka, Sprite, some grenadine, and a cherry on top. *A bit girly*, I thought, keeping my face straight.

"A Naughty Shirley for the man of the hour," he said, handing the completed drink across the bar to Jack. Jack took a big sip and let out a sigh of happiness.

"Best bartender ever," he said, winking at me.

"The woman upstairs didn't say anything about having someone else," I said. The bar was barely big enough to hold both of us. We were going to be running into one another all night. Taking another look at him, though, I didn't really mind that idea.

"The guys brought me in special. I used to be their bartender when we were in college." Noah grinned at me.

"All right." I grinned back and pulled out an empty beer pitcher. I had a couple of crumpled ones in my pocket that I threw in it and set it out on the counter. "What side of the bar do you want?"

"I'll take this side," Noah said, inclining his head to the left.

"Barkeep!" Jack called out. "Sex on the Beach next, if you don't mind."

"You know, you really have to buy me dinner first," Noah told him with a wink, pulling out a bottle of peach schnapps. Despite being a seasoned bartender, hearing the words "sex on the beach" come from the mouth of a devastatingly handsome man made my insides tingle.

"Make me an Angel's Tit, Noah." The blonde man Jack had been talking to leaned up against the bar. I snickered slightly.

"Any real drinks?" I teased.

"With these two?" Noah laughed. "Not likely. The reason I was their favorite bartender was because I was the only one who could make the drinks girly enough for them!"

I giggled, already feeling the energy of the night. Jack tossed a five dollar bill into the tip jar after Noah handed him his drink. I grinned at him. With guests like these, the night was going to be hilarious- and profitable.

"So," I said, pulling out the crème de cocao for Noah

to make the blonde man's drink. "You're Noah, you're Jack, the guy at the door is Dean, and you are?" I looked expectantly at the handsome blonde man. If I knew their names, I would make better tips.

The three men looked at one another, silent for a second, and then started laughing.

"You don't know who he is?" Noah asked in disbelief.

"No..." I frowned and looked at him closer. He looked slightly familiar, but given that he was Hollywood movie-star handsome, it was probably that I had seen him on TV. "Should I?"

"This is my house. Jack here is just borrowing it." The blonde man smiled. I felt his eyes practically burn into me, daring me to remember. "Does that help?"

Think, think... "I got nothing."

The three men laughed again, and somehow they seemed to relax even more.

"Bob. His name's Bob," Jack grinned. "I guess you don't know Noah's or my last names?"

"If I didn't know his first name, how the heck am I supposed to know your last names?" I reasoned with him. His grin got bigger. "Why, are you guys famous or something?"

"Or something," Noah said, handing "Bob" his completed Angel's Tit. "Bob" tossed a ten dollar bill into the tip jar.

Two more men entered the man cave, getting past Hawaiian-shirt Bodyguard Dean with a nod. One was tall and slender with messy honey-colored curls that looked perfect for tangling fingers in. The other was portly and pale, the lines of his face suggesting that the sour look was his usual, permanent expression. His suit looked expensive, but it didn't fit him right and it looked out of place among the other guests' casual t-shirts and shorts.

"Joe!" Jack called out, hurrying over to shake the

attractive man's hand. "Joe" got a very confused look on his face.

"Dude, this is Paul..." "Joe" said, patting Jack's shoulder as if he were a confused child. "You've met him before."

Jack rolled his eyes. "No, *you're* Joe. Our bartender doesn't know who we are." Jack grinned as "Joe's" eyes lit up as he got it.

"The fake name game? I love it. I guess he's still Paul, then." "Joe" inclined his head at the heavy-set man bee-lining his way to the bar. "Who's everybody else?"

"I already introduced myself as Jack. Same with Noah. But "Bob" did not."

"Lucky Bob, then. Noah's here? Awesome." Joe turned to the bar, and I felt his eyes do a once over down my body. "Lucky Noah, actually." At least the last part was quiet enough that I could imagine he hadn't meant me to hear it.

"Give me some of that 1954 Mccallan scotch, sweetheart," Paul said." And don't be stingy." His eyes slid down the opening of my shirt like he owned me. I fought the urge to button up. Hopefully he tipped as well as his friends.

I poured him a generous glass of the amber liquid and set it on the counter. He took one small sip, a smile crossing his thin lips before slamming the rest of it down. I tried not to look horrified. Scotch, especially a bottle that probably cost around three grand, should not be slammed back like a shot. It would be like using a Monet as toilet paper.

"One more, honey," Paul rasped. He coughed slightly at the alcohol burning his esophagus. I guess when you had rich friends, it was tempting to use their nice things in a way you wouldn't normally. I tried to forgive him a little, but it was hard. "If you want some fun later..." He winked and dropped a quarter in the tip jar.

I poured a modest glass, and this time he picked it up and sipped rather than chugging. He gave me that thin-lipped smile that made my stomach curdle a little and went to sit on the couch with "Joe" and "Bob." Jack was starting up a game of some sort on the giant TV screen. Paul turned down an offer for a controller, looking at the black plastic like it might bite him.

"Don't mind him," Noah said, leaning up on the bar beside me. "He's usually pretty harmless. I can't believe Lo--I mean "Joe"--brought him, though."

"He's not a friend of Jack's?" I asked, wiping down the empty Naughty Shirley glass.

"Not really." Noah shook his head. "He's a lawyer. He's helped us all out at some point or another. I'm just surprised he came. This isn't exactly his type of party."

I looked over at the man on the couch, sipping away on his scotch and glaring at the TV. I could see him at a loud club, leering at the girls, and telling them all how terribly important he was. Sitting on a couch with a bunch of barely-thirty-somethings playing *Halo* didn't exactly fit him.

I shook the beer pitcher, rattling the quarter from Paul. "At least he's a good tipper."

Noah laughed, putting his hand on my shoulder. It was like sexual lighting hit me. Heat flooded my stomach, and if I were less of a lady and more a caveman, I would have thrown him over my shoulder and found a bedroom somewhere. I had no idea it was even possible to have that strong a connection just by someone casually touching my shoulder.

I glanced up at Noah, wondering if he felt it too, but he just smiled down at me like he was actually just interested in the tip jar. Except those eyes. They held a blue fire that told me he had felt something too, despite what the rest of his face said.

He cleared his throat, releasing my shoulder and getting a cup of Malibu and Coke for himself. "So, you live here on the island?"

"Yeah." I grabbed one for myself. Rachel *did* say to have a good time. "You just here for the party?"

Noah nodded. "I'm here for a couple of days. My schedule is pretty open, though."

"If you want, I'd be happy to show you around the island. I mean, if "Bob" doesn't want the honor," I offered. Noah's face split into a grin. He nodded and opened his mouth to speak, but a new guest cut him off.

Available Exclusively on Amazon

ABOUT THE AUTHOR

Krista Lakes is a newly turned 30 year old who recently rediscovered her passion for writing. She loves aquatic life and running marathons. She is living happily ever after with her Prince Charming and her bouncing baby boy.

Krista would love to hear from you! Please contact her at Krista.Lakes@gmail.com or like her on Facebook!